REFLECTIONS ON THE DEATH OF A PORCUPINE

REFLECTIONS ON THE DEATH OF A PORCUPINE AND OTHER ESSAYS

By

D. H. LAWRENCE

A Midland Book

INDIANA UNIVERSITY PRESS

BLOOMINGTON • LONDON

First Midland Book edition, 1963
With the permission of the Estate of the late Frieda Lawrence
All Rights Reserved
pa. ISBN 0-253-20043-1

3   4   5   6   7   79   7⁸   77   7⁶   75

CONTENTS

❧

THE CROWN

NOTE TO THE CROWN

The Crown was written in 1915, when the war was already twelve months old, and had gone pretty deep. John Middleton Murry said to me: "Let us do something."

The doing consisted in starting a tiny monthly paper, which Murry called The Signature, and in having weekly meetings somewhere in London—I have now no idea where it was—up a narrow stair-case over a green-grocer's shop: or a cobbler's shop. The only thing that made any impression on me was the room over the shop, in some old Dickensey part of London, and the old man downstairs.

We scrubbed the room and colour-washed the walls and got a long table and some windsor chairs from the Caledonian market. And we used to make a good warm fire: it was dark autumn, in that unknown bit of London. Then on Thursday nights we had meetings of about a dozen people. We talked, but there was absolutely nothing in it. And the meetings didn't last two months.

The Signature was printed by some little Jewish printer away in the east end. We sold it by subscription, half-a-

crown for six copies. I don't know how many subscriptions there were: perhaps fifty. The helpless little brown magazine appeared three times, then we dropped it. The last three of the Crown essays were never printed.

To me the venture meant nothing real: a little escapade. I can't believe in "doing things" like that. In a great issue like the war, there was nothing to be "done", in Murry's sense. There is still nothing to be "done". Probably not for many, many years will men start to "do" something. And even then, only after they have changed gradually, and deeply.

I knew then, and I know now, it is no use trying to do anything—I speak only for myself—publicly. It is no use trying merely to modify present forms. The whole great form of our era will have to go. And nothing will really send it down but the new shoots of life springing up and slowly bursting the foundations. And one can do nothing, but fight tooth and nail to defend the new shoots of life from being crushed out, and let them grow. We can't make life. We can but fight for the life that grows in us.

So that, personally, little magazines mean nothing to me: nor groups, nor parties of people. I have no hankering after quick response, nor the effusive, semi-intimate back-chat of literary communion. So it was ridiculous to offer The Crown in a little six-penny pamphlet. I always felt ashamed, at the thought of the few who sent their half-crowns. Happily they were few; and they could read Murry. If one publishes in the ordinary way, people are not asked for their sixpences.

I alter The Crown only a very little. It says what I still believe. But it's no use for a five minutes' lunch.

THE CROWN

I

THE LION AND THE UNICORN
WERE FIGHTING FOR THE CROWN

WHAT is it then, that they want, that they are forever rampant and unsatisfied, the king of beasts and the defender of virgins? What is this Crown that hovers between them, unattainable? Does either of them ever hope to get it?

But think of the king of beasts lying serene with the crown on his head! Instantly the unicorn prances from every heart. And at the thought of the lord of chastity with the crown ledged above his golden horn, lying in virgin lustre of sanctity, the lion springs out of his lair in every soul, roaring after his prey.

It is a strange and painful position, the king of beasts and the beast of purity, rampant for ever on either side of the crown. Is it to be so for ever?

Who says lion?—who says unicorn? A lion, a lion!! Hi, a unicorn! Now they are at it, they have forgotten all about the crown. It is a greater thing to have an enemy than to have an object. The lion and the unicorn were fighting, it is no question any more of the crown. We know this, because when the lion beat the unicorn, he did not take the crown and put it on his head, and say, "Now Mr. Purity, I'm king". He drove the unicorn out of town, expelled him, obliterated him, expurgated him from the memory, exiled him from the kingdom. Instantly the town was all lion, there was no unicorn at all, no scent nor flavour of unicorn.

"Unicorn!" they said in the city. "That is a mythological beast that never existed."

There was no question any more of rivalry. The unicorn was erased from the annals of fact.

Why did the lion fight the unicorn? Why did the unicorn fight the lion? Why must the one obliterate the other? Was it the *raison d'être* of each of them, to obliterate the other?

But think, if the lion really destroyed, killed the unicorn: not merely drove him out of town, but annihilated him! Would not the lion at once expire, as if he had created a vacuum around himself? Is not the unicorn necessary to the very existence of the lion, is not each opposite kept in stable equilibrium by the opposition of the other.

This is a terrible position: to have for a *raison d'être* a purpose which, if once fulfilled, would of necessity entail the cessation from existence of both opponents. They would both cease to be, if either of them really won in the fight which is their sole reason for existing. This is a troublesome thought.

It makes us at once examine our own hearts. What do we find there?—a want, a need, a crying out, a divine discontent. Is it the lion, is it the unicorn?—one, or both? But certainly there is this crying aloud, this infant crying in the night, born into a blind want.

What do we find at the core of our hearts?—a want, a void, a hollow want. It is the lion that must needs fight the unicorn, the unicorn that must needs fight the lion. Supposing the lion refuses the obligation of his being, and says, "I won't fight, I'll just lie down. I'll be a lion couchant."

What *then* is the lion? A void, a hollow ache, a want. "What am I?" says the lion, as he lies with his head between his paws, or walks by the river feeding on raspberries, peacefully, like a unicorn. "I am a hollow void, my roaring is the resonance of a hollow drum, my strength is the power of the vacuum, drawing all things within itself."

Then he groans with horrible self-consciousness. After all, there is nothing for it but to set upon the unicorn, and so forget, forget, obtain the precious self-oblivion.

Thus are we, then, rounded upon a void, a hollow

want, like the lion. And this want makes us draw all things into ourselves, to fill up the void. But it is a bottomless pit, this void. If ever it were filled, there would be a great cessation from being, of the whole universe.

Thus we portray ourselves in the field of the royal arms. The whole history is the fight, the whole *raison d'être*. For the whole field is occupied by the lion and the unicorn. These alone are the living occupants of the immortal and mortal field.

We have forgotten the Crown, which is the keystone of the fight. We are like the lion and the unicorn, we go on fighting underneath the Crown, entirely oblivious of its supremacy.

It is modest common sense for us to acknowledge, all of us, nowadays, that we are built round a void and hollow want which, if satisfied, would imply our collapse, our utter ceasing to be. Therefore we regard our craving with complacence, we feel the great aching of the Want, and we say, with conviction, "I know I exist, I know I am I, because I feel the divine discontent which is personal to me, and eternal, and present always in me."

That is because we are incomplete, we stand upon one side of the shield, or on the other. On the one side we are in darkness, our eyes gleam phosphorescent like cat's eyes. And with these phosphorescent gleaming eyes we look across at the opposite pure beast, and we say, "Yes, I am a lion, my *raison d'être* is to devour that unicorn, I am moulded upon an eternal void, a Want." Gleaming bright, we see ourselves reflected upon the surface of the darkness and we say: "I am the pure unicorn, it is for me to oppose and resist for ever that avid lion. If he ceased to exist, I should be supreme and unique and perfect. Therefore I will destroy him."

But the lion will not be destroyed. If he were, if he were swallowed into the belly of the unicorn, the unicorn would fly asunder into chaos.

This is like being a creature who walks by night, who says: "Men see by darkness, and in the darkness they have their being." Or like a creature that walks by day, and says: "Men live by the light."

We are enveloped in the darkness, like the lion: or like the unicorn, enveloped in the light.

For the womb is full of darkness, and also flooded with the strange white light of eternity. And we, the peoples of the world, we are enclosed within the womb of our era, we are there begotten and conceived, but not brought forth.

A myriad, myriad people, we roam in the belly of our era, seeking, seeking, wanting. And we seek and want deliverance. But we say we want to overcome the lion that shares with us this universal womb, the walls of which are shut, and have no window to inform us that we are in prison. We roam

[5]

within the vast walls of the womb, unnourished now, because the time of our deliverance is ripe, even overpast, and the body of our era is lean and withered because of us, withered and inflexible.

We roam unnourished, moulded each of us around a core of want, a void. We stand in the darkness of the womb and we say: "Behold, there is the light, the white light of eternity, which we want." And we make war upon the lion of darkness, annihilate him, so that we may be free in the eternal light. Or else, suddenly, we admit ourselves the lion, and we rush rampant on the unicorn of chastity.

We stand in the light of Virginity, in the wholeness of our unbroached immortality, and we say: "Lo the darkness surrounds us, to envelop us. Let us resist the powers of darkness." Then like the bright and virgin unicorn we make war upon the ravening lion. Or we cry: "Ours is the strength and glory of the Creator, who precedes Creation, and all is unto us." So we open a ravening mouth, to swallow back all time has brought forth.

And there is no rest, no cessation from the conflict. For we are two opposites which exist by virtue of our inter-opposition. Remove the opposition and there is collapse, a sudden crumbling into universal nothingness.

The darkness, this has nourished us. The darkness, this is a vast infinite, an origin, a Source. The Beginning, this is the great sphere of darkness, the womb wherein the universe is begotten.

But this universal, infinite darkness conceives of its own opposite. If there is universal, infinite darkness, then there is universal, infinite light, for there cannot exist a specific infinite save by virtue of the opposite and equivalent specific infinite. So that if there be universal, infinite darkness in the beginning, there must be universal, infinite light in the end. And these are two relative halves.

Into the womb of the primary darkness enters the ray of ultimate light, and time is begotten, conceived, there is the beginning of the end. We are the beginning of the end. And there, within the womb, we ripen upon the beginning, till we become aware of the end.

We are fruit, we are an integral part of the tree. Till the time comes for us to fall, and we hang in suspense, realising that we are an integral part of the vast beyond, which stretches under us and grasps us even before we drop into it.

We are the beginning, which has conceived us within its womb of darkness, and nourished us to the fulness of our growth. This is ours that we adhere to. This is our God, Jehovah, Zeus, the Father of Heaven, this that has conceived and created us, in the beginning, and brought us the fulness of our strength.

And when we have come to the fulness of our strength, like lions which have been fed till they are full grown, then the strange necessity comes upon us, we must travel away, roam like falling fruit, fall from the initial darkness of the tree, of the cave which has reared us, into the eternal light of germination and begetting, the eternal light, shedding our darkness like the fruit that rots on the ground.

We travel across between the two great opposites of the Beginning and the End, the eternal night and everlasting day, and the transit is a stride taken, the night gives us up for the day to receive us. And what are we between the two?

But before the transit is accomplished, whilst we are yet like fruit heavy and ripe on the trees, we realise the delirious freedom of the end, the goal, and we cry: "Behold, I, who am here within the darkness, I am the light! I am the light, I am Unicorn, the beam of chastity. Behold, the beam of Virginity gleams within my loins, in this circumambient darkness. Behold, I am not the Beginning, I am the End. The End is universal light, the achieving again of infinite unblemished being, the infinite oneness of the Light, the escape from the infinite not-being of the darkness."

All the time, these cries take place within the womb, these are the myriad unborn uttering themselves as they come towards maturity, cry after cry as the darkness develops itself over the sea of Light, and flesh is born, and limbs; cry after cry as the light develops within the darkness, and mind is born, and the consciousness of that which is outside my own flesh and limbs, and the desire for everlasting life grows more insistent.

These are the cries of the two adversaries, the two opposites.

First of all the flesh develops in splendour and glory out of the prolific darkness, begotten by the light it develops to a great triumph, till it dances naked in glory of itself, before the Ark, naked in glory of itself in the procession of heroes travelling towards the wise goddess, the white light, the Mind, the light which the vessel of living darkness has caught and captured within itself, and holds in triumph. The flesh of darkness triumphant circles round the treasure of light which it has enveloped, which it calls Mind, and this is the ecstasy, the dance before the Ark, the Bacchic delirium.

And then, within the womb, the light grows stronger and finds voice, it cries out: "Behold, I am free, I am not enveloped within this darkness. Behold, I am the everlasting light, the Eternity that stretches forward for ever, utterly the opposite of that darkness which departs backward, backward for ever. Come over to me, to the light, to the light that streams into the glorious eternity. For now the darkness is revoked for ever."

THE CROWN

It is the voice of the unicorn crying in the wilderness, it is the Son of Man. And behold, in the fight, the unicorn beats the lion, and drives him out of town.

But all of this is within the Womb. The darkness builds up the warm shadow of the flesh in splendour and triumph, enclosing the light. This is the zenith of David and Solomon, and of Assyria and Egypt. Then the light, wrestling within the vessel, throws up a white gleam of universal love, which is St. Francis of Assisi, and Shelley.

Then each has reached its maximum of self-assertion. The flesh is made perfect within the womb, the spirit is at last made perfect also, within the womb. They are equally perfect, equally supreme, the one adhering to the infinite darkness of the beginning, the other adhering to the infinite light of the end.

Yet, within the womb, they are eternally opposite. Darkness stands over against light, light stands over against dark. The lion is reared against the unicorn, the unicorn is reared against the lion. One says, "Behold, the darkness which gave us birth is eternal and infinite: this we belong to." The other says, "We are of the Light, which is everlasting and infinite."

And there is no reconciliation, save in negation. From the present, the stream flows in opposite directions, back to the past, on to the future. There are two goals, at opposite ends of time. There is the vast original dark out of which Creation issued, there is the Eternal light into which all mortality passes. And both are equally infinite, both are equally the goal, and both equally the beginning.

And we, fully equipped in flesh and spirit, fully built up of darkness, perfectly composed out of light, what are we but light and shadow lying together in opposition, or lion and unicorn fighting, the one to vanquish the other. This is our eternal life, in these two eternities which nullify each other. And we, between them both, what are we but nullity?

And this is because we see in part, always in part. We are enclosed within the womb, we are the seed from the loins of the eternal light, or we are the darkness which is enveloped by the body of the past, by our era.

Unless the sun were enveloped in the body of darkness, would a cast shadow run with me as I walk? Unless the night lay within the embrace of light, would the fish gleam phosphorescent in the sea, would the light break out of the black coals of the hearth, would the electricity gleam out of itself, suddenly declaring an opposite being?

Love and power, light and darkness, these are the temporary conquest of the one infinite by the other. In love, the Christian love, the End asserts itself supreme: in power, in strength like the lion's the Beginning re-establishes itself unique. But when the opposition is complete on either side, then there is perfection. It is the perfect opposition of dark and light that brindles the tiger with gold flame and dark flame. It is the surcharge of darkness that opens the ravening mouth of the tiger, and drives his eyes to points of phosphorescence. It is the perfect balance of light and darkness that flickers in the stepping of a deer. But it is the conquered darkness that flares and palpitates in her eyes.

There are the two eternities fighting the fight of Creation, the light projecting itself into the darkness, the darkness enveloping herself within the embrace of light. And then there is the consummation of each in the other, the consummation of light in darkness and darkness in light, which is absolute: our bodies cast up like foam of two meeting waves, but foam which is absolute, complete, beyond the limitation of either infinity, consummate over both eternities. The direct opposites of the Beginning and the End, by their very directness, imply their own supreme relation. And this supreme relation is made absolute in the clash and the foam of the meeting waves. And the clash and the foam are the Crown, the Absolute.

The lion and the unicorn are not fighting for the Crown. They are fighting beneath it. And the Crown is upon their fight. If they made friends and lay down side by side, the Crown would fall on them both and kill them. If the lion really beat the unicorn, then the Crown pressing on the head of the king of beasts alone would destroy him. Which it has done and is doing. As it is destroying the unicorn who has achieved supremacy in another field.

So that now, in Europe, both the lion and the unicorn are gone mad, each with a crown tumbled on his bound-in head. And without rhyme or reason they tear themselves and each other, and the fight is no fight, it is a frenzy of blind things dashing themselves and each other to pieces.

Now the unicorn of virtue and virgin spontaneity has got the Crown slipped over the eyes, like a circle of utter light, and has gone mad with the extremity of light: whilst the lion of power and splendour, its own Crown of supreme night settled down upon it, roars in an agony of imprisoned darkness.

Now within the withered body of our era, within the husk of the past, the seed of light has come to supreme self-consciousness and has gone mad with the flare of eternal light in its eyes, whilst the fruit of darkness, unable to fall from the tree, has turned round towards the tree and is become mad, clinging faster upon the utter night whence it should have dropped away long ago.

For the stiffened, exhausted, inflexible loins of our era are too dry to give us forth in labour, the tree is withered, we are pent in, fastened, and now have turned round, some to the source of darkness, some to the source of light, and gone mad, purely given up to frenzy. For the dark has travelled to the light, and the light towards the dark. But when they reached the bound, neither could leap forth. The fruit could not fall from the tree, the lion just full grown could not get out of the cave, the unicorn could not enter the illimitable forest, the lily could not leap out of the darkness of her bulb straight into the sun. What then? The road was stopped. Whither then? Backward, back to the known eternity. There was a great, horrible huddle backwards. The process of birth had been arrested, the inflexible, withered loins of the mother-era were too old and set, the past was taut around us all. Then began chaos, the going asunder, the beginning of nothingness. Then we leaped back, by reflex from the bound and limit, back upon ourselves into madness.

There is a dark beyond the darkness of the womb, there is a light beyond the light of knowledge. There is the darkness of all the heavens for the seed of man to invest, and the light of all the heavens for the womb to receive. But we don't know it. How can the unborn within the womb know of the heavens outside; how can they?

How can they know of the tides beyond? On the one hand murmurs the utter, infinite sea of darkness, full of unconceived creation: on the other the infinite light stirs with eternal procreation. They are two seas which eternally attract and oppose each other, two tides which eternally advance to repel each other, which foam upon one another, as the ocean foams on the land, and the land rushes down into the sea.

And we, in the great movement, are begotten, conceived and brought forth, like the waves which meet and clash and burst up into foam, sending the foam like light, like shadow, into the zenith of the absolute, beyond the grasp of either eternity.

We are the foam and the foreshore, that which, between the oceans, is not, but that which supersedes the oceans in utter reality, and gleams in absolute Eternity.

The Beginning is-not, nor the eternity which lies behind us, save in part. Partial also is the eternity which lies in front. But that which is not partial, but whole, that which is not relative, but absolute, is the clash of the two into one, the foam of being thrown up into consummation.

It is the music which comes when the cymbals clash one upon the other: this is absolute and timeless. The cymbals swing back in one or the other direction of time, towards one or the other relative eternity. But absolute, timeless, beyond time or eternity, beyond space or infinity, is the music that was the consummation of the two cymbals in opposition.

THE CROWN

It is that which comes when night clashes on day, the rainbow, the yellow and rose and blue and purple of dawn and sunset, which leaps out of the breaking of light upon darkness, of darkness upon light, absolute beyond day or night; the rainbow, the iridescence which is darkness at once and light, the two-in-one; the crown that binds them both.

It is the lovely body of foam that walks for ever between the two seas, perfect and consummate, the revealed consummation, the oneness that has taken being out of the two.

We say the foam is evanescent, the wind passes over it and it is gone—he who would save his life must lose it.

But if indeed the foam were-not, if the two seas fell apart, if the sea fell departed from the land, and the land from the sea, if the two halves, day and night, were ripped asunder, without attraction or opposition, what then? Then there would be between them nothingness, utter nothingness. Which is meaningless.

So that the foam and the iridescence, the music that comes from the cymbals, all formed things that come from perfect union in opposition, all beauty and all truth and being, all perfection, these are the be-all and the end-all, absolute, timeless, beyond time or eternity, beyond the Limit or the Infinite.

This lovely body of foam, this iris between the

two floods, this music between the cymbals, this truth between the surge of facts, this supreme reason between conflicting desires, this holy spirit between the opposite divinities, this is the Absolute made visible between the two Infinities, the Timelessness into which are assumed the two Eternities.

It is wrong to try to make the lion lie down with the lamb. This is the supreme sin, the unforgivable blasphemy of which Christ spoke. This is the creating of nothingness, the bringing about, or the striving to bring about the nihil which is pure meaninglessness.

The great darkness of the lion must gather into itself the little, feeble darkness of the lamb. The great light of the lamb must absorb elsewhere, in the whole world, the small, weak light of the lion. The lamb indeed will inherit the world, rather than the lion. It is the triumph of the meek, but the meek, like the merciless, shall perish in their own triumph. Anything that *triumphs*, perishes. The consummation comes from perfect relatedness. To this a man may *win*. But he who triumphs, perishes.

The crown is upon the perfect balance of the fight, it is not the fruit of either victory. The crown is not prize of either combatant. It is the *raison d'être* of both. It is the absolute within the fight.

And those alone are evil, who say, "The lion shall lie down with the lamb, the eagle shall mate with the dove, the lion shall munch in the stable of the unicorn." For they blaspheme against the *raison d' être* of all life, they try to destroy the essential, intrinsic nature of God.

But it is the fight of opposites which is holy. The fight of like things is evil. For if a thing turn round upon itself in blind frenzy of destruction, this is to say: "The lamb shall roar like the lion, the dove strike down her prey like the eagle, and the unicorn shall devour the innocent virgin in her path". Which is precisely the equivalent blasphemy to the blasphemy of universal meekness, or peace.

And this, this last, is our blasphemy of the war. We would have the lamb roar like the lion, all doves turn into eagles.

II

LIFE is a travelling to the edge of knowledge, then a leap taken. We cannot know beforehand. We are driven from behind, always as over the edge of the precipice.

It is a leap taken, into the beyond, as a lark leaps into the sky, a fragment of earth which travels to be fused out, sublimated, in the shining of the heavens.

But it is not death. Death is neither here nor there. Death is a temporal, relative fact. In the absolute, it means nothing. The lark falls from the sky and goes running back to her nest. This is the ebb of the wave. The wave of earth flung up in spray, a lark, a cloud of larks, against the white wave of the sun. The spray of earth and the foam of heaven are one, consummated, a rainbow mid-way, a song. The larks return to earth, the rays go back to heaven. But these are only the shuttles that weave the iris, the song, mid-way, in absoluteness, timelessness.

[19]

THE CROWN

Out of the dark, original flame issues a tiny green flicker, a weed coming alive. On the edge of the bright, ultimate, spiritual flame of the heavens is revealed a fragment of iris, a touch of green, a weed coming into being. The two flames surge and intermingle, casting up a crest of leaves and stems, their battlefield, their meeting-ground, their marriage bed, the embrace becomes closer, more unthinkably vivid, it leaps to climax, the battle grows fiercer, fiercer, intolerably, till there is the swoon, the climax, the consummation, the little yellow disk gleams absolute between heaven and earth, radiant of both eternities, framed in the two infinities. Which is a weed, a sow-thistle bursting into blossom. And we, the foreshore in whom the waves of dark and light are unequally seething, we can see this perfection, this absolute, as time opens to disclose it for a moment, like the Dove that hovered incandescent from heaven, before it is closed again in utter timelessness.

"But the wind passeth over it and is gone."

The wind passes over it and we are gone. It is time which blows in like a wind, closing up the clouds again upon the perfect gleam. It is the wind of time, out of either eternity, a wind which has a source and an issue, which swirls past the light of this absolute, like waves past a lighted buoy. For the light is not temporal nor eternal, but absolute. And we, who are temporal and eternal, at moments only we cease from our temporality. In these, our moments, we see the sow-thistle gleaming, light within darkness, darkness within light, consummated, we are with the song and the iris.

And then it is we, not the iris, not the song, who are blown away. We are blown for a moment against the yellow light of the window, the flower, then on again into the dark turmoil.

We have made a mistake. We are like travellers travelling in a train, who watch the country pass by and pass away; all of us who watch the sun setting, sliding down into extinction, we are mistaken. It is not the country which passes by and fades, it is not the sun which sinks to oblivion. Neither is it the flower that withers, nor the song that dies out.

It is we who are carried past in the seethe of mortality. The flower is timeless and beyond condition. It is we who are swept on in the condition of time. So we shall be swept as long as time lasts. Death is part of the story. But we have being also in timelessness, we shall become again absolute, as we have been absolute, as we are absolute.

We know that we are purely absolute. We know in the last issue we are absolved from all opposition. We know that in the process of life we are purely relative. But timelessness is our fate, and time is subordinate to our fate. But time is eternal.

And the life of man is like a flower that comes into

blossom and passes away. In the beginning, the light touches the darkness, the darkness touches the light, and the two embrace. They embrace in opposition, only in their desire is their unanimity. There are two separate statements, the dark wants the light, and the light wants the dark. But these two statements are contained within the one: "They want each other." And this is the condition of absoluteness, this condition of their wanting each other, that which makes light and dark consummate even in opposition. The interrelation between them, this is constant and absolute, let it be called love or power or what it may. It is all the things that it can be called.

In the beginning, light touches darkness and darkness touches light. Then life has begun. The light enfolds and implicates and involves the dark, the dark receives and interpenetrates the light, they come nearer, they are more finely combined, till they burst into the crisis of oneness, the blossom, the utter being, the transcendent and timeless flame of the iris.

Then time passes on. Out of the swoon the waves ebb back, dark towards the dark, light towards the light. They ebb back and away, the leaves return unto the darkness of the earth, the quivering glimmer of substance returns into the light, the green of the last wavering iris disappears, the waves ebb apart, further, further, further.

THE CROWN

Yet they never separate. The whole flood recedes, the tides are going to separate. And they separate entirely, save for one enfolded ripple, the tiny, silent, scarce-visible enfolded pools of the seeds. These lie potent, the meeting-ground, the well-head wherein the tides will surge again, when the turn comes.

This is the life of man. In him too the tide sweeps together towards the utter consummation, the consummation with the darkness, the consummation with the light, flesh and spirit, one culminating crisis, when man passes into timelessness and absoluteness.

The residue of imperfect fusion and unfulfilled desire remains, the child, the well-head where the tides will flow in again, the seed. The absolute relation is never fully revealed. It leaps to its maximum of revelation in the flower, the mature life. But some of it rolls aside, lies potent in the enfolded seed. My desire is fulfilled, I, as individual am become timeless and absolute, perfect. But the whole desire of which I am part remains yet to be consummated. In me the two waves clash to perfect consummation. But immediately upon the clash come the next waves of the tide rippling in, the ripples, forerunners, which tinily meet and enfold each other, the seed, the unborn child. For we are all waves of the tide. But the tide contains all the waves.

It may happen that waves which meet and mingle come to no consummation, only a confusion and a swirl and a falling away again. These are the myriad lives of human beings which pass in confusion of nothingness, the uncreated lives. There are myriads of human lives that are not absolute nor timeless, myriads that just waver and toss temporarily, never become more than relative, never come into being. They have no being, no immortality. There are myriads of plants that never come to flower, but which perish away for ever, always separated in the fringe of time, never united, never consummated, never brought forth.

I know I am compound of two waves, I, who am temporal and mortal. When I am timeless and absolute, all duality has vanished. But whilst I am temporal and mortal, I am framed in the struggle and embrace of the two opposite waves of darkness and of light.

There is the wave of light in me which seeks the darkness, which has for its goal the Source and the Beginning, for its God the Almighty Creator to Whom is all power and glory. Thither the light of the seed of man struggles and aspires, into the infinite darkness, the womb of all creation.

What way is it that leads me on to the Source, to the Beginning? It is the way of the blood, the way of power. Down the road of the blood, further and further into the darkness, I come to the Almighty God Who was in the beginning, is now, and ever shall be. I come to the Source of Power. I am received back into the utter darkness of the Creator, I am once again with Him.

This is a consummation, a becoming eternal. This is an arrival into eternity. But eternity is only relative.

I can become one with God, consummated into eternity, by taking the road down the senses into the utter darkness of power, till I am one with the darkness of initial power, beyond knowledge of any opposite.

It is thus, seeking consummation in the utter darkness, that I come to the woman in desire. She is the doorway, she is the gate to the dark eternity of power, the creator's power. When I put my hand on her, my heart beats with a passion of fear and ecstasy, for I touch my own passing away, my own ceasing-to-be, I apprehend my own consummation in a darkness which obliterates me in its infinity. My veins rock as if they were being destroyed, the blood takes fire on the edge of oblivion, and beats backward and forward. I resist, yet I am compelled; the woman resists, yet she is compelled. And we are the relative parts dominated by the strange compulsion of the absolute.

Gradually my veins relax their gates, gradually the rocking blood goes forward, quivers on the edge of oblivion, then yields itself up, passes into the borderland of oblivion. Oh, and then I would die, I would quickly die, to have all power, all life at once, to come instantly to pure, eternal oblivion, the source of life. But patience is fierce at the bottom of me; fierce, indomitable, abiding patience. So my blood goes forth in shock after shock of delirious passing-away, in shock after shock entering into consummation, till my soul is slipping its moorings, my mind, my will fuses down, I melt out and am gone into the eternal darkness, the primal creative darkness reigns, and I am not, and at last *I am*.

Shock after shock of ecstasy and the anguish of ecstasy, death after death of trespass into the unknown, till I fall down into the flame, I lapse into the intolerable flame, a pallid shadow I am transfused into the flux of unendurable darkness, and am gone. No spark nor vestige remains within the supreme dark flow of the flame, I am contributed again to the immortal source. I am with the dark Almighty of the beginning.

Till, new-created, I am thrown forth again on the shore of creation, warm and lustrous, goodly, new born from the darkness out of which all time has issued.

And then, new-born on the knees of darkness, new-issued from the womb of creation, I open my eyes to the light and know the goal, the end, the light which stands over the end of the journey, the everlasting day, the oneness of the spirit.

THE CROWN

The new journey, the new life has begun, the travelling to the opposite eternity, to the infinite light of the Spirit, the consummation in the Spirit.

My source and issue is in two eternities, I am founded in the two infinities. But absolute is the rainbow that goes between; the iris of my very being.

It may be, however, that the seed of light never propagates within the darkness, that the light in me is sterile, that I am never re-born within the womb, the Source, to be issued towards the opposite eternity.

It may be there is a great inequality, disproportion, within me, that I am nearly all darkness, like the night, with a few glimmers of cold light, moonlight, like the tiger with white eyes of reflected light brindled in the flame of darkness. Then I shall return again and again to the womb of darkness, avid, never satisfied, my spirit will fall unfertile into the womb, will never be conceived there, never brought forth. I shall know the one consummation, the one direction only, into the darkness. It will be with me for ever the almost, almost, almost, of satisfaction, of fulfilment. I shall know the one eternity, the one infinite, the one immortality, I shall have partial being; but never the whole, never the full. There is an infinite which does not know me. I am always relative, always partial, always, in the last issue, unconsummate.

THE CROWN

The barren womb can never be satisfied, if the quick of darkness be sterile within it. But neither can the unfertile loins be satisfied, if the seed of light, of the spirit, be dead within them. They will return again and again and again to the womb of darkness, asking, asking, and never satisfied.

Then the unconsummated soul, unsatisfied, uncreated in part, will seek to make itself whole by bringing the whole world under its own order, will seek to make itself absolute and timeless by devouring its opposite. Adhering to the one eternity of darkness, it will seek to devour the eternity of light. Realising the one infinite of the Source, it will endeavour to absorb into its oneness the opposite infinite of the Goal. This is the infinite with its tail in its mouth.

Consummated in one infinite, and one alone, this soul will assert the oneness of all things, that all things are one in the One Infinite of the Darkness, of the Source. One is one and all alone and ever more shall be so. This is the cry of the Soul consummated in one eternity only.

There is one eternity, one infinite, one God. "Thou shalt have no other god before me."

But why this Commandment, unless there were in truth another god, at least the equal of Jehovah?

Consummated in the darkness only, having not enough strength in the light, the partial soul cries out in a convulsion of insistence that the darkness alone is infinite and eternal, that all light is from the small, contained sources, the lamps lighted at will by the desire of the Creator, the sun, the moon and stars. These are the lamps and candles of the Almighty, which He blows out at will. These are little portions of special darkness, darkness transfigured, these lights.

There is one God, one Creator, one Almighty; there is one infinite and one eternity, it is the infinite and the eternity of the Source. There is One Way: it is the Way of the Law. There is one Life, the Life of Creation, there is one Goal, the Beginning, there is one immortality, the immortality of the great I Am. All is God, the One God. Those who deny this are to be stamped out, tortured, tortured for ever.

It is possible then to deny it?

Having declared the One God, then the partial soul, fulfilled of the darkness only, proceeds to establish this God on earth, to devour and obliterate all else.

Rising from the darkness of consummation in the flesh, with the woman, it seeks to establish its kingdom over all the world. It strides forth, the lord, the master, strong for mastery. It will dominate all, all, it will bring all under the rules of itself, of the One, the Darkness lighted with the lamps of its own choice.

THE CROWN

This is the heroic tyrant, the fabulous king-warrior, like Sardanapolus or Caesar, like Saul even. These warrior kings seek to pass beyond all relatedness, to become absolute in might and power. And they fall inevitably. Their Judas is a David, a Brutus: the individual who knows something of both flames, but commits himself to neither. He holds himself, in his own ego, superior either to the creative dark power-flame, or the conscious love-flame. And so, he is the small man slaying the great. He is virtuous egoistic Brutus, or David: David slaying the preposterous Goliath, overthrowing the heroic Saul, taking Bathsheba and sending Uriah to death: David dancing naked before the Ark, asserting the oneness, his own oneness, the one infinity, *himself*, the egoistic God, I AM. And David never went in unto Michal any more, because she jeered at him. So that she was barren all her life.

But it was David who really was barren. Michal, when she mocked, mocked the sterility of David. For the spirit in him was blasted with unfertility; he could not become born again, he could not be conceived in the spirit. Michal, the womb of profound darkness, could not conceive to the overweak seed of David's spirit. David's seed was too impure, too feeble in sheer spirit, too egoistic, it bred and begot preponderant egoists. The flood of vanity set in after David, the lamps and candles began to gutter.

THE CROWN

Power is sheer flame, and spirit is sheer flame, and between them is the clue of the Holy Ghost. But David put a false clue between them: the clue of his own ego, cunning and *triumphant*.

It is unfertility of spirit which sends man raging to the woman, and sends him raging away again, unsatisfied. It is not the woman's barrenness: it is his own. It is sterility in himself which makes a Don Juan.

And the course of the barren spirit is dogmatically to assert One God, One Way, One Glory, one exclusive salvation. And this One God is indeed God, this one Way is the way, but it is the way of egoism, and the One God is the reflection, inevitably, of the worshipper's ego.

This is the sham Crown, which the victorious lion and the victorious unicorn alike puts on his own head. When either *triumphs*, the true crown disappears, and the triumphant puts a false crown on his own head: the crown of sterile egoism. The true Crown is above the fight itself, and above the embrace itself, not upon the brow of either fighter or lover. Or, if you like, in the true fight it shines equally upon the brow of the defeated and the winner. For sometimes, it is blessed to be beaten in a fight.

He who triumphs, perishes. As Caesar perished, and Napoleon. In the fight they were wonderful, and the power was with them. But when they would be supreme, sheer triumphers, exalted in their own ego, then they fell. Triumph is a false absolution, the winner salutes his enemy, and the light of victory is on *both* their brows, since both are consummated.

In the same way, Jesus triumphant perished. Any individual who will triumph, in love or in war, perishes. There is no triumph. There is but consummation in either case.

So Shelley also perishes. He wants to be love triumphant, as Napoleon wanted to be power triumphant. Both fell.

In both, there is the spuriousness of the *ego* trying to seize the Crown that belongs only to the consummation.

In the Roman "Triumph" itself lay the source of Rome's downfall. And in the arrogance of England's dispensation of Liberty in the world lies the downfall of England. When Liberty triumphs, as in Russia, where then is the British Empire? Where then is the British Lion, crowned *Fidei Defensor*, Defender of the Faith of Liberty and Love? When liberty needs no more defending, then the protective lion had better look out.

Take care of asserting any absolute, either of power or love, of empire or democracy. The moment power *triumphs*, it becomes spurious with sheer egoism, like Caesar and Napoleon. And the moment democracy triumphs, it too becomes hideous with egoism, like Russia now.

Either lion or unicorn, triumphant, turns into a sheer beast of prey. Foe it has none: only prey—or victims.

So we have seen in the world, every time that power has triumphed: every time the lion and the eagle have jammed the crown down on their heads. Now it will be given us to see democracy triumphant, the unicorn and the dove seizing the crown, and on the instant turning into beasts of prey.

The true crown is upon the consummation itself, not upon the triumph of one over another, neither in love nor in power. The ego is the false absolute. And the ego crowned with the crown is the monster and the tyrant, whether it represent one man, an Emperor, or a whole mass of people, a Demos. A million egos summed up under a crown are not *better* than one individual crowned ego. They are a million times worse.

III

THE FLUX OF CORRUPTION

THE tiger blazed transcendent into immortal darkness. The unique phoenix of the desert grew up to maturity and wisdom. Sitting upon her tree, she was the only one of her kind in all creation, supreme, the zenith, the perfect aristocrat. She attained to perfection, eagle-like she rose in her nest and lifted her wings, surpassing the zenith of mortality; so she was translated into the flame of eternity, she became one with the fiery Origin.

It was not for her to sit tight, and assert her own tight ego. She was gone as she came.

In the nest was a little ash, a little flocculent grey dust wavering upon a blue-red, dying coal. The red coal stirred and gathered strength, gradually it grew white with heat, it shot forth sharp gold flames. It was the young phoenix within the nest, with curved beak growing hard and crystal, like a scimitar, and talons hardening into pure jewels.

[34]

THE CROWN

Wherein, however, is the immortality, in the constant occupation of the nest, the widow's cruse, or in the surpassing of the phoenix? She goes gadding off into flame, into her consummation. In the flame she is timeless. But the ash within the nest lies in the restless hollow of time, shaken on the tall tree of the desert. It will rise to the same consummation, become absolute in flame.

In a low, shady bush, far off, on the other side of the world, where the rains are cold and the mists wrap the leaves in a chillness, the ring-dove presses low on the bough, while her mate sends forth the last ru-cuooo of peace. The mist darkens and ebbs-in in waves, the trees are melted away, all things pass into a universal oneness, with the last re-echoing dove, peace, all pure peace, ebbing in softer, softer waves to a universal stillness.

The dark blue tranquillity is universal and infinite, the doves are asleep in the sleeping boughs, all fruits are fallen and are silent and cold, all the leaves melt away into pure mist of darkness.

It is strange, that away on the other side of the world, the tiger gleams through the hot-purple darkness, and where the dawn comes crimson, the phoenix lifts her wings in a yawn like an over-sumptuous eagle, and passes into flame above the golden palpable fire of the desert.

Here are the opposing hosts of angels, the ruddy

choirs, the upright, rushing flames, the lofty Cherubim that palpitate about the Presence, the Source; and then the tall, still angels soft and pearly as mist, who await round theGoal, the attendants that hover on the edge of the last Assumption.

And from the seed two travellers set forth, in opposite directions, the one concentrating towards the upper, ruddy, blazing sun, the zenith, the creative fire; the other towards the blue, cold silence, dividing itself and ever dividing itself till it is infinite in the universal darkness.

And at the summit, the zenith, there is a flash, a flame, as the traveller enters into infinite, there is a red splash as the poppy leaps into the upper, fiery eternity. And far below there is unthinkable silence as the roots ramify and divide and pass into the oneness of unutterable silence.

The flame is gone, the flower has leapt away, the fruit ripens and falls. Then dark ebbs back to dark, and light to light, hot to hot, and cold to cold. This is death and decay and corruption. And the worm, the maggot, these are the ministers of separation, these are the tiny clashing ripples that still ebb together, when the chief tide has set back, to flow utterly apart.

This is the terror and wonder of dark returning to dark, and of light returning to light, the two departing back to their Sources. This we cannot bear to think of. It is the temporal flux of corruption, as the flux together was the temporal flux of creation. The flux is temporal. It is only the perfect meeting, the perfect interpenetration into oneness, the kiss, the blow, the two-in-one, that is timeless and absolute.

And dark is not willing to return to dark till it has known the light, nor light to light till it has known the dark, till the two have been consummated into oneness. But the act of death may itself be a consummation, and life may be a state of negation.

It may be that our state of life is itself a denial of the consummation, a prevention, a negation; that this life is our nullification, our not-being.

It may be that the flower is held from the search of the light, and the roots from the dark, like a plant that is pot-bound. It may be that, as in the autumnal cabbage, the light and the dark are made prisoners in us, their opposition is overcome, the ultimate moving has ceased. We have forgotten our goal and our end. We have enclosed ourselves in our exfoliation, there are many little channels that run out into the sand.

This is evil, when that which is temporal and relative asserts itself eternal and absolute. This I, which I am, has no being save in timelessness. In my consummation, when that which came from the Beginning and that which came from the End are transfused into oneness, then I come into being, I have existence. Till then I am only a part of nature; I am not.

But as part of nature, as part of the flux, I have my instrumental identity, my inferior I, myself-conscious ego.

If I say that *I am*, this is false and evil. I am not. Among us all, how many have being?—too few. Our ready-made individuality, our identity is no more than an accidental cohesion in the flux of time. The cohesion will break down and utterly cease to be. The atoms will return into the flux of the universe. And that unit of cohesion which I was will vanish utterly. Matter is indestructible, spirit is indestructible. This of us remains, in any case, general in the flux. But the soul that has not come into being has no being for ever. The soul does not come into being at birth. The soul comes into being in the midst of life, just as the phoenix in her maturity becomes immortal in flame. That is not her perishing: it is her becoming absolute: a blossom of fire. If she did not pass into flame, *she* would never really exist. It is by her translation into fire that she is the phoenix. Otherwise she were only a bird, a transitory cohesion in the flux.

It is absurd to talk about all men being immortal, all having souls. Very few men have being at all. They perish utterly, as individuals. Their endurance afterwards is the endurance of Matter within the flux, non-individual : and spirit within the flux. Most men are just transitory natural phenomena. Whether they live or die does not matter: except in so far as every failure in the part is a failure in the whole. Their death is of no more matter than the cutting of a cabbage in the garden, an act utterly apart from grace.

They assert themselves as important, as absolute mortals. They are just liars. When one cuts a fat autumnal cabbage, one cuts off a lie, to boil it down in the pot.

They are all just fat lies, these people, these many people, these mortals. They are innumerable cabbages in the regulated cabbage plot. And our great men are no more than Mrs. Wiggs of the Cabbage Patch.

The cabbage is a nice fat lie. That is why we eat it. It is the business of the truthful to eat up the lies. A fatted cow is a lie, and a fat pig is a lie, and a fatted sheep is a lie, just the same: these sacrificial beasts, these lambs and calves, become fat lies when they are merely protected and fed full.

The cabbage is a lie because it asserts itself as a permanency, in the state wherein it finds itself. In the swirl of the Beginning and the End, stalk and leaves take place. But the stalk and leaves are only the swirl of the waves. Yet they say, they are absolute, they have achieved a permanent form. It is a lie. Their universal absolute is only the far-off dawning of the truth, the false dawn which in itself is nothing, nothing except in relation to that which comes after.

But they say, "We are the consummation and the reality, we are the fulfilment." This is pure amorphousness. Each one becomes a single, separate entity, a single separate nullity. Having started along the way to eternity, they say, "We are there, we have arrived," and they enclose themselves in the nullity of the falsehood.

And this is the state of man, when he falls into self-sufficiency, and asserts that his self-conscious ego is It. He falls into the condition of fine cabbages.

Then they are wealthy and fat. They go no further, so they become wealthy. All that great force which would carry them naked over the edge of time, into timelessness, into being, they convert into fatness, into having. And they are full of self-satisfaction. Having no being, they assert their artificial completeness, and the life within them becomes a will-to-have; which is the expression of the will-to-persist, in the temporary unit. Selfishness is the subjugating of all things to a false entity, and riches is the great flux over the edge of the bottomless pit, the falsity, the nullity. For where is the rich man who is not the very bottomless pit? Travel nearer, nearer, nearer to him, and one comes to the gap, the hole, the abyss where his soul should be. He is not. And to stop up his hollowness, he drags all things unto himself.

And what are we all, all of us, collectively, even the poorest, now, in this age? We are only potentially rich men. We are all alike. The distinction between rich and poor is purely accidental. Rich and poor alike are only, each one, a pit-head surrounding the bottomless pit. But the rich man, by pouring vast quantities of matter down his void, gives himself a more pleasant illusion of fulfilment than the poor man can get: that is all. Yet we would give our lives, every one of us, for this illusion.

There are no rich or poor, there are no masses and middle classes and aristocrats. There are myriads of framed gaps, people, and a few timeless fountains, men and women. That is all.

Myriads of framed gaps! Myriads of little egos, all wearing the crown of life! Myriads of little Humpty-Dumpties, self-satisfied emptinesses, all about to have a great fall.

The current ideal is to be a gap with a great heap of matter around it, which can be sent clattering down. The most sacred thing is to give all your having so that it can be put on the heaps that surround all the other bottomless pits. If you give away all your having, even your life, then, you are a bottomless pit with no sides to it. Which is infinite. So that to become infinite, give away all your having, even to your life. So that you will achieve immortality yourself. Like the heroes of the war, you will become the bottomless pit itself; but more than this, you will be contributing to the public good, you will be one of those who make blessed history: which means, you will be heaping goods upon the dwindling heaps of superfluity that surrounds these bottomless lives of the myriad people. If we poor can each of us hire a servant, then the servant will be like a stone tumbling always ahead of us down the bottomless pit. Which creates an almost perfect illusion of having a solid earth beneath us.

Long ago we agreed that we had fulfilled all purpose and that our only business was to look after other people. We said; "It is marvellous, we are really complete." If the regulation cabbage, hidebound and solid, could walk about on his stalk, he would be very much as we are. He would think of himself as we think of ourselves, he would talk, as we talk, of the public good.

But inside him, proper and fine, the heart would be knocking and urgent, the heart of the cabbage. Of course for a long time he would not hear it. His good, enveloping green leaves outside, the heap round the hole, would have closed upon him very early, like Wordsworth's "Shades of the prison house," very close and complete and gratifying.

But the heart would beat within him, beat and beat, grow louder and louder, till it was threshing the whole of his inside rotten, threshing him hollow, till his inside began to devour his consciousness.

Then he would say: "I must do something." Looking round he would see little dwindly cabbages struggling in the patch, and would say: "So much injustice, so much suffering and poverty in the world, it cannot be." Then he would set forth to make dwindly cabbages into proper, fine cabbages. So he would be a reformer.

He would kick, kick, kick against the conditions which make some cabbages poor and dwindly, most cabbages poorer and more dwindly than himself. He would but be kicking against the pricks.

But it is very profitable to kick against the pricks. It gives one a sensation, and saves one the necessity of bursting. If our reformers had not had the prickly wrongs of the poor to kick, so that they hurt their toe quite sorely, they might long ago have burst outwards from the enclosed form in which we have kept secure.

Let no one suffer, they have said. No mouse shall be caught by a cat, no mouse. It is a transgression. Every mouse shall become a pet, and every cat shall lap milk in peace, from the saucer of utter benevolence.

This is the millennium, the golden age that is to be, when all shall be domesticated, and the lion and the leopard and the hawk shall come to our door to lap milk and to peck the crumbs, and no sound shall be heard but the lowing of fat cows and the baa-ing of fat sheep.

THE CROWN

This is the Green Age that is to be, the age of the perfect cabbage. This was our hope and our fulfilment, for this, in this hope, we lived and we died.

So the virtuous, public-spirited ones have suffered bitterly from the aspect of their myriad more-or-less blighted neighbors, whom they love as themselves. They have lived and died to right the wrong conditions of social injustice.

Meanwhile the threshing has continued at the core of us, till our entrails are threshed rotten. We are a wincing mass of self-consciousness and corruption, within our plausible rind. The most unselfish, the most humanitarian of us all, he is the hollowest and fullest of rottenness. The more rotten we become, the more insistent and insane becomes our desire to ameliorate the conditions of our poorer, and maybe healthier neighbours.

Fools, vile fools! Why cannot we acknowledge and admit the horrible pulse and thresh of corruption within us. What is this self-consciousness that palpitates within us like a disease? What is it that threshes and threshes within us, drives us mad if we see a cat catch a sparrow?

We dare not know. Oh, we are convulsed with shame long before we come to the point. It is indecent beyond endurance to think of it.

Yet here let it be told. It was the living desire for immortality, for being, which urged us ceaselessly.

THE CROWN

It was the bud within the cabbage, threshing, threshing, threshing. And now, oh our convulsion of shame, when we must know this! We would rather die.

Yet it shall be made known. It was the struggling of the light and darkness within us, towards consummation, towards absoluteness, towards flowering. Oh, we shriek with anger of shame as the truth comes out: that the cabbage is rotten within because it wanted to straddle up into weakly fiery flower, wanted to straddle forth in a spire of ragged, yellow, inconsequential blossom.

Oh God, it is unendurable, this revelation, this disclosure, it is not to be borne. Our souls perish in an agony of self-conscious shame, we will not have it.

Yet had we listened, the hide-bound cabbage might have burst, might have opened apart, for a venturing forth of the tender, timid, ridiculous cluster of aspirations, that issue in little yellow tips of flame, the flowers naked in eternity, naked above the staring unborn crowd of amorphous entities, the cabbages: the myriad egos.

But the crowd of assertive egos, of tough entities, they were too strong, too many. Quickly they extinguished any shoot of tender immortality from among them, violently they adhered to the null rind and to the thresh of rottenness within.

Still the living desire beat and threshed at the

heart of us, relentlessly. And still the fixed will of the temporal form we have so far attained, the static, mid-way form, triumphed in assertion.

Still the false I, the ego, held down the real, un-born I, which is a blossom with all a blossom's fragility.

Yet constantly the rising flower pushed and thrust at the belly and heart of us, thrashed and beat relent-lessly. If it could not beat its way through into be-ing, it must thrash us hollow. Let it do so then, we said. This also we enjoy, this being threshed rotten inside. This is sensationalism, reduction of the com-plex tissue back through rottenness to its elements. And this sensationalism, this reduction back, has be-come our very life, our only form of life at all. We enjoy it, it is our lust.

It became at last a collective activity, a war, when, within the great rind of virtue we thresh destruction further and further, till our whole civilization is like a great rind full of corruption, of breaking down, a mere shell threatened with collapse upon itself.

And the road of corruption leads back to one eter-nity. The activity of utter going apart has, in eter-nity, a result equivalent to the result of utter coming together. The tiger rises supreme, the last brindled flame upon the darkness; the deer melts away, a blood-stained shadow received into the utter pallor of light; each having leapt forward into eternity, at opposite extremes. Within the closed shell of the Christian conception, we lapse utterly back, through reduction, back to the Beginning. It is the triumph of death, of decomposition.

And the process is that of the serpent lying prone in the cold, watery fire of corruption, flickering with the flowing-apart of the two streams. His belly is white with the light flowing forth from him, his back is dark and brindled where the darkness returns to the Source. He is the ridge where the two floods flow apart. So in the orange-speckled belly of the newt, the light is taking leave of the darkness, and returning to the light; the imperious, demon-like crest is the flowing home of the darkness. He is the god within the flux of corruption, from him proceeds the great retrogression back to the Beginning and back to the End. These are our gods.

There are elsewhere the golden angels of the Kiss, the golden, fiery angels of strife, those that have being when we come together, as opposites, as complements coming to consummation. There is delight and triumph elsewhere, these angels sound their loud trumpets. Then men are like brands that have burst spontaneously into flame, the phoenix, the tiger, the glistening dove, the white-burning unicorn.

But here are only the angels that cleave asunder, terrible and invincible. With cold, irresistible hands they put us apart, they send like unto like, darkness unto darkness. They thrust the seas backward from embrace, backward from the locked strife. They set the cold phosphorescent flame of light flowing back to the light, and cold heavy darkness flowing back to the darkness. They are the absolute angels of corruption, they are the snake, the newt, the water-lily, as reflected from below.

I cease to be, my darkness lapses into utter, stone darkness, my light into a light that is keen and cold as frost.

This goes on within the rind. But the rind remains permanent, falsely absolute, my false absolute self, my self-conscious ego. Till the work of corruption is finished; then the rind also, the public form, the civilization, the established consciousness of mankind disappears as well in the mouth of the worm, taken unutterably asunder by the hands of the angels of separation. It ceases to be, all the civilization and all the consciousness, it passes utterly away, a temporary cohesion in the flux. It was this, this rind, this persistent temporary cohesion, that was evil, this alone was evil. And it destroys us all before itself is destroyed.

IV

WITHIN the womb of the established past, the light has entered the darkness, the future is conceived. It is conceived, the beginning of the end has taken place. Light is within the grip of darkness, darkness within the embrace of light, the Beginning and the End are closed upon one another.

They come nearer and nearer, till the oneness is full grown within the womb of the past, within the belly of Time, it must move out, must be brought forth, into timelessness.

But something withholds it. The pregnancy is accomplished, the hour of labour has come. Yet the labour does not begin. The loins of the past are withered, the young unborn is shut in.

All the time, within the womb, light has been travelling to the dark, the interfusion of the two into a oneness has continued. Now that it is fulfilled,

[49]

it meets with some arrest. It is the dry walls of the womb which cannot relax.

There is a struggle. Then the darkness, having overcome the light, reaching the dead null wall of the womb, reacts into self-consciousness, and recoils upon itself. At the same time the light has surpassed its limit, become conscious, and starts in reflex to recoil upon itself. Thus the false I comes into being: the I which thinks itself supreme and infinite, and which is, in fact, a sick foetus shut up in the walls of an unrelaxed womb.

Here, at this moment when the birth pangs should begin, when the great opposition between the old and the young should take place, when the young should beat back the old body that surrounds it, and the old womb and loins should expel the young body, there is a deadlock. The two cannot fight apart. The walls of the old body are inflexible and insensible, the unborn does not know that there can be any travelling forth. It conceives itself as the whole universe, surrounded by dark nullity. It does not know that it is in prison. It believes itself to have filled up the whole of the universe, right to the extremes where is nothing but blank nullity.

It is tremendously conceited. It can only react upon itself. And the reaction can only take the form of self-consciousness. For the self is everything, universal, the surrounding womb is just the outer darkness in which that which *is*, exists. Therefore there remains either to die, to pass into the outer darkness, or to enter into self-knowledge.

So the unborn recoils upon itself, dark upon dark, light upon light. This is the horror of corruption begun already within the unborn, already dissolution and corruption set in before birth. And this is the triumph of the ego.

Mortality has usurped the Crown. The unborn, reacting upon the null walls of the womb, assumes that it has reached the limit of all space and all being. It concludes that its self is fulfilled, that all consummation is achieved. It takes for certain that itself has filled the whole of space and the whole of time.

And this is the glory of the ego.

There is no more fight to be fought, there is no more to be sought and embraced. All is fought and overcome, all is embraced and contained. It is all concluded, there is nothing remaining but the outer nothingness, the only activity is the reaction against the outer nothingness, into the achieved being of the self, all else is fulfilled and concluded. To die is merely to assume nothingness. The limit of all life is reached.

And this is the apotheosis of the ego.

So there is the great turning round upon the self, dark upon dark, light upon light, the flux of separation, corruption within the unborn. The tides which are set towards each other swirl back as from a promontory which intervenes. There has been no consummation. There can be no consummation. The only thing is to return, to go back—that which came from the Beginning to go back to the Beginning, that which came from the End to return to the End. In the return lies the fulfilment.

And this is the unconscious undoing of the ego.

That which we *are* is absolute. There is no adding to it, no superseding this accomplished self. It is final and universal. All that remains is thoroughly to explore it.

That is, to analyse it. Analysis presupposes a corpse.

It is at this crisis in the human history that tragic art appears again, that art becomes the only absolute, the only watchword among the people. This achieved self, which we are, is absolute and universal. There is nothing beyond. All that remains is to state this self, and the reactions upon this self, perfectly. And the perfect statement presumes to be art. It is aestheticism.

At this crisis there is a great cry of loneliness. Every man conceives himself as a complete unit surrounded by nullity. And he cannot bear it. Yet his pride is in this also. The greatest conceit of all is the cry of loneliness.

At this crisis, emotion turns into sentiment, and sentimentalism takes the place of feeling. The ego has no feeling, it has only sentiments. And the myriad egos sway in tides of sentimentalism.

But the *tacit* utterance of every man, when this state is reached, is *"Après moi le Déluge."* And when the deluge begins to set in, there is profound secret satisfaction on every hand. For the ego in a man secretly hates every other ego. In a democracy where every little ego is crowned with the false crown of its own supremacy, every other ego is a false usurper, and nothing more. We can only tolerate those whose crowns are not yet manufactured, because they can't *afford* it.

And again, the supreme little ego in man hates an unconquered universe. We shall never rest till we have heaped tin cans on the North Pole and the South Pole, and put up barb-wire fences on the moon. Barb-wire fences are our sign of conquest. We have wreathed the world with them. The back of creation is broken. We have killed the mysteries and devoured the secrets. It all lies now within our skin, within the ego of humanity.

So circumscribed within the outer nullity, we give ourselves up to the flux of death, to analysis, to introspection, to mechanical war and destruction, to humanitarian absorption in the body politic, the poor, the birth-rate, the mortality of infants, like a man absorbed in his own flesh and members, looking for ever at himself. It is the continued activity of disintegration—disintegration, separating, setting apart, investigation, research, the resolution back to the original void.

All this goes on within the glassy, insentient, insensible envelope of nullity. And within this envelope, like the glassy insects within their rind, we imagine we fill the whole cosmos, that we contain within ourselves the whole of time, which shall tick forth from us as from a clock, now everlastingly.

We are capable of nothing but reduction within the envelope. Our every activity is the activity of disintegration, of corruption, of dissolution, whether it be our scientific research, our social activity—(the social activity is largely concerned with reducing all the parts contained within the envelope to an equality, so that there shall be no unequal pressure, tending to rupture the envelope, which is divine)—our art, or our anti-social activity, sensuality, sensationalism, crime, war. Everything alike contributes to the flux of death, to corruption, and liberates the static data of the consciousness.

Whatever single act is performed by any man now, in this condition, it is an act of reduction, disintegration. The scientist in his laboratory, the artist in his study, the statesman, the artisan, the sensualist obtaining keen gratification, every one of these is reducing down that which is himself to its simpler elements, reducing the compound back to its parts. It is the pure process of corruption in all of us. The activity of death is the only activity. It is like the decay of our flesh, and every new step in decay liberates a sensation, keen, momentarily gratifying, or a conscious knowledge of the parts that made a whole; knowledge equally gratifying.

It is like Dmitri Karamazov, who seeks and experiences sensation after sensation, reduction after reduction, till finally he is stripped utterly naked before the police, and the quick of him perishes. There *is* no more any physical or integral Dmitri Karamazov. That which is in the hospital, afterwards, is a conglomeration of qualities, strictly an idiot, a nullity.

And Dostoevsky has shown us perfectly the utter subjection of all human life to the flux of corruption. That is his theme, the theme of reduction through sensation after sensation, consciousness after consciousness, until nullity is reached, all complexity is broken down, an individual becomes an amorphous heap of elements, qualities.

There are the two types, the dark Dmitri Karamazov, or Rogozhin; and the Myshkin on the other hand. Dmitri Karamazov and Rogozhin will each of them plunge the flesh within the reducing agent, the woman, obtain the sensation and the reduction within the flesh, add to the sensual experience, and progress towards utter dark disintegration, to nullity. Myshkin on the other hand will react upon the achieved consciousness or personality or ego of every one he meets, disintegrate this consciousness, this ego, and his own as well, obtaining the knowledge of the factors that made up the complexity of the consciousness, the ego, in the woman and in himself, reduce further and further back, till himself is a babbling idiot, a vessel full of disintegrated parts, and the woman is reduced to a nullity.

This is real death. The actual physical fact of death is part of the life-stream. It is an incidental point when the flux of light and dark has flowed sufficiently apart for the conjunction, which we call life, to disappear.

We live with the pure flux of death, it is part of us all the time. But our blossoming is transcendent, beyond death and life.

Only when we fall into egoism do we lose all chance of blossoming, and then the flux of corruption is the breath of our existence. From top to bottom, in the whole nation, we are engaged, fundamentally engaged in the process of reduction and dissolution. Our reward is sensational gratification in the flesh, or sensational gratification within the mind, the utter gratification we experience when we can pull apart the whole into its factors. This is the reward in scientific and introspective knowledge, this is the reward in the pleasure of cheap sensuality.

In each case, the experience remains as it were

absolute. It is the statement of what is, or what was. And a statement of what *is*, is the absolute footstep in the progress backward towards the starting place, it is the *undoing* of a complete unit into the factors which previously went to making its oneness. It is the reduction of the iris back into its component waves.

There was the bliss when the iris came into being. There is now the bliss when the iris passes out of being, and the whole is torn apart. The secret of the whole is never captured. Certain data are captured. The secret escapes down the sensual, or the sensational, or intellectual, thrill of pleasure.

So there goes on reduction after reduction within the shell. And we, who find our utmost gratification in this process of reduction, this flux of corruption, this retrogression of death, we will preserve with might and main the glassy envelope, the insect rind, the tight-shut shell of the cabbage, the withered, null walls of the womb. For by virtue of this null envelope alone do we proceed uninterrupted in this process of gratifying reduction.

And this is utter evil, this secret, silent worship of the null envelope that preserves us intact for our gratification with the flux of corruption.

Intact within the null envelope, which we have come to worship as the preserver of this our life-activity of reduction, we re-act back upon what we are. We do not seek any more the consummation of union. We seek the consummation of reduction.

When a man seeks a woman in love, or in positive desire, he seeks a union, he seeks a consummation of himself with that which is not himself, light with dark, dark with light.

But within the glassy, null envelope of the enclosure, no union is sought, no union is possible; after a certain point, only reduction. Ego reacts upon ego only in friction. There are small egos, many small people, who have not reached the limit of the confines which we worship. They may still have small consummation in union. But all those who are strong and have travelled far have met and reacted from the nullity.

And then, when a man seeks a woman, he seeks not a consummation in union, but a frictional reduction. He seeks to plunge his compound flesh into the cold acid that will reduce him, in supreme sensual experience, down to his parts. This is Rogozhin seeking Nastasia Filippovna, Dmitri his Grushenka, or D'Annunzio in Fuoco seeking his Foscarina. This is more or less what happens when a soldier, maddened with lust of pure destructiveness, violently rapes the woman of his captivity. It is that he may destroy another being by the very act which is called the act of creation, or procreation. In the brute soldier it is cruelty-lust: as it was in the Red Indian.

THE CROWN

But when we come to civilized man, it is not so simple. His cruelty-lust is directed almost as much against himself as against his victim. He is destroying, reducing, breaking down that of himself which is within the envelope. He is immersing himself within a keen, fierce, terrible reducing agent. This is true of the hero in Edgar Allan Poe's tales, *Ligeia*, or the *Fall of the House of Usher*. The man seeks his own sensational reduction, but he disintegrates the woman even more, in the name of love. In the name of love, what horrors men perpetrate, and are applauded!

It is only in supreme crises that man reaches the supreme pitch of annihilation. The difference, however, is only a difference in degree, not in kind. The bank-clerk performs in a mild degree what Poe performed intensely and deathlily.

These are the men in whom the development is rather low, whose souls are coarsely compounded, so that the reduction is coarse, a sort of activity of coarse hate.

But the men of finer sensibility and finer development, sensuous or conscious, they must proceed more gradually and subtly and finely in the process of reduction. It is necessary for a finely compounded nature to reduce itself more finely, to know the subtle gratification of its own reduction.

A subtle nature like Myshkin's would find no pleasure of reduction in connection with Grushenka, scarcely any with Nastasia. He must proceed more delicately. He must give up his soul to the reduction. It is his mind, his conscious self he wants to reduce. He wants to dissolve it back. He wants to become infantile, like a child, to reduce and resolve back all the complexity of his consciousness, to the rudimentary condition of childhood. That is his ideal.

So he seeks mental contacts, mental re-actions. It is in his mental or conscious contacts that he seeks to obtain the gratification of self-reduction. He reaches his crisis in his monologue of self-analysis, self-dissolution, in the drawing-room scene where he falls in a fit.

And of course, all this reducing activity is draped in alluring sentimentalism. The most evil things in the world, today, are to be found under the chiffon folds of sentimentalism. Sentimentality is the garment of our vice. It covers viciousness as inevitably as greenness covers a bog.

With all our talk of advance, progress, we are all the time working backwards. Our heroines become younger and younger. In the movies, the heroine is becoming more and more childish, and touched with infantile idiocy. We cannot bear honest maturity. We want to reduce ourselves back, back to the *corruptive* state of childishness.

Now it is all very well for a child to be a child. But for a grown person to be slimily, pornigraphically reaching out for child-gratifications, is disgusting. The same with the prevalent love of boys. It is the desire to be reduced back, reduced back, in our accomplished ego: always within the unshattered rind of our completeness and complacency, to go backwards, in sentimentalised disintegration, to the states of childhood.

And no matter *what* happens to us, now, we sentimentalise it and use it as a means of sensational reduction. Even the great war does not alter our civilization one iota, in its total nature. The form, the whole form, remains intact. Only inside the complete envelope we writhe with sensational experiences of death, hurt, horror, reduction.

The goodness of anything depends on the direction in which it is moving. Childhood, like a bud, striving and growing and struggling towards blossoming full maturity, is surely beautiful. But childhood as a *goal*, for which grown people aim: childishness futile and sentimental, for which men and women lust, and which always retreats when grasped, like the *ignis fatuus* of a poisonous marsh of corruption: this is disgusting.

While we live, we are balanced between the flux of life and the flux of death. All the while our bodies are being composed and decomposed. But while every man fully lives, all the time the two streams keep fusing into the third reality, of real creation.

THE CROWN

Every new gesture, every fresh smile of a child is a new emergence into creative being: a glimpse of the Holy Ghost.

But when grown people start grimacing with childishness, or lusting after child-gratifications, it is corruption pure and simple.

And the still clear look on an old face, and the stillness of old, withered hands, which have gathered the long repose of autumn, this is the purity of the two streams consummated, and the bloom, like autumn crocuses, of age.

But the painted, silly child-face that old women make nowadays: or the harpy's face that many have, lusting for the sensations of youth: the hard, voracious, selfish faces of old men, seeking their own ends, devouring the shoots of young life: this is vile.

While we live, we are balanced between the flux of life and the flux of death. But the real clue is the Holy Ghost, that moves us on into the state of blossoming. And each year the blossoming is different: from the delicate blue speedwells of childhood to the equally delicate, frail farewell flowers of old age: through all the poppies and sunflowers: year after year of difference.

While we live, we change, and our flowering is a constant change.

But once we fall into the state of egoism, we cannot change. The ego, the self-conscious ego remains fixed, a final envelope around us. And we are then safe inside the mundane egg of our own self-consciousness and self-esteem.

Safe we are! Safe as houses! Shut up like unborn chickens that cannot break the shell of the egg. That's how safe we are! And as we can't be born, we can only rot. That's how safe we are!

Safe within the everlasting walls of the egg-shell we have not the courage, nor the energy, to crack, we fall, like the shut-up chicken, into a pure flux of corruption, and the worms are our angels.

And mankind falls into the state of innumerable little worms bred within the unbroken shell: all clamoring for food, food, food, all feeding on the dead body of creation, all crying peace! peace! universal peace! brotherhood of man! Everything must be "universal", to the conquering worm. It is only *life* which is different.

V

THE NUPTIALS OF DEATH AND THE ATTENDANT VULTURE

TO THOSE who are in prison, whose being is prisoner within the walls of unliving fact, there are only two forms of triumph: the triumph of inertia, or the triumph of the Will. There is no flowering possible. And the experience *en route* to either triumph, is the experience of sensationalism.

Stone walls need not a prison make: that is, not an *absolute* prison. If the great sun has shone into a man's soul, even prison-walls cannot blot it out. Yet prison-walls, unless they be a temporary shelter are deadly things.

So, if we are imprisoned within walls of accomplished fact, experience, or knowledge, we are prisoned indeed. The living sun is shut out finally. A false sun, like a lamp, shines.

All absolutes are prison-walls. These "laws" which science has invented, like conservation of energy, indestructibility of matter, gravitation, the will-to-live, survival of the fittest: and even these absolute facts, like—the earth goes round the sun, or the doubtful atoms, electrons, or ether—they are all prison-walls, unless we realise that we don't know what they mean. We don't know what we mean, ultimately, by *conservation*, or *indestructibility*. Our atoms, electrons, ether, are caps that fit exceeding badly. And our will-to-live contains a germ of suicide, and our survival-of-the-fittest the germ of degeneracy. As for the earth going round the sun: it goes round as the blood goes round my body, absolutely mysteriously, with the rapidity and hesitation of life.

But the human ego, in its pettifogging arrogance, sets up these things for you as absolutes, and unless you kick hard and kick in time, they are your prison walls forever. Your spirit will be like a dead bee in a cell.

Once you are in prison, you have no experience left, save the experience of reduction, destruction going on inwardly. Your sentimentalism is only the smell of your own rottenness.

This reduction within the self is sensationalism. And sensationalism, of course, is progressive. You can't have your cake and eat it. To get a sensation, you eat your cake. That is, to get a sensation, you reduce down some part of your complex psyche, physical and psychic. You get a flash, as when you strike a match. But a match once struck can never be struck again. It is finished—sensationalism is an exhaustive process.

The resolving down is progressive. It can apparently go on *ad infinitum*. But in infinity it means what we call utter death, utter nothingness, opposites released from opposition, and from conjunction, till there *is* nothing left at all, only nullity itself.

Sensationalism progresses in the individual. This is the doom of it. This is the doom of egoistic sex. Egoistic sex-excitement means the reacting of the sexes against one another in a purely reducing activity. The reduction progresses. When I have finally reduced one complexity, one unit, I must proceed to the next, the lower. It is the progressive activity of dissolution within the soul.

And the climax of this progression is in perversity, degradation and death. But only the very powerful and energetic ego can go through all the phases of its own violent reduction. The ordinary crude soul, after having enjoyed the brief reduction in the sex, is finished there, blasé, empty. And alcohol is slow and crude, and opium is only for the imaginative, the somewhat spiritual nature. Then remain the opium-drugs, for a finisher, a last reducer.

There remains only the reduction of the contact with death. So that as the sex is exhausted, gradually, a keener desire, the desire for the touch of death follows on, in an intense nature. Then come the fatal drugs. Or else those equally fatal wars and revolutions which really create nothing at all, but destroy, and leave emptiness.

When a man is cleaving like a fly with spread arms upon the face of a rock, with infinite space beneath him, and he feels his foothold going, and he cries out to the men on the rope, and falls away, dangling into endless space, jerked back by the thin rope, then he perishes, he is fused in the reducing flame of death. He knows another keen anguish of reduction. What matters to that man, afterwards? Does any of the complex life of the world below matter? None. All that is left is the triumph of his will in having gone so far and recovered. And all that lies ahead is another risk, another slip, another agony of the fall, or a demonish triumph of the will. And the *final* consummation of such a man is the last fall of all, the few horrible seconds whilst he drops, like a meteorite, to extinction. This is his final and utter satisfaction, the smash of extinction at the bottom.

But even this man is not a pure egoist. This man still has his soul open to the mystery of the mountains, he still feels the passion of the *contact* with death.

If he wins, however, in the contest: if his will triumphs in the test: then there is danger of his falling into final egoism, the more-or-less inert complacency of a self-satisfied old man.

THE CROWN

The soul is still alive, while it has passion: any sort of passion, even for the brush with death, or for the final and utter reduction. And in the brush with death it may be released again into positive life. A man may be sufficiently released by a fall on the rope and the dangling for a few minutes of agony, in space. That may finally reduce his soul to its elements, set it free and child-like, and break-down that egoistic entity which has developed upon it from the past. The near touch of death may be a release into life; if only it will break the egoistic will, and release that other flow.

But if a man, having fallen very near to death, gets up at length and says: "I did it! It's my triumph! I beat the mountains that time!"—then, of course, his ego has only pulled itself in triumph out of the menace, and the individual will go on more egoistic and barrenly complacent.

If a man says: "I fell! But the unseen goodness helped me, when I struggled for life, and so I was saved"—then this man will go on in life unimprisoned, the channels of his heart open, and passion still flowing through him.

But if the brush with death only gave the brilliant sensational thrill of fear, followed immediately, by the *gamin* exultance: "Yah! I got myself out all right!"—then the ego continues intact, having enjoyed the sensation, and remaining vulgarly triumphant in the power of the Will. And it will continue inert and complacent till the next thrill.

So it is with war. Whoever goes to war in his own might alone, will even if he come out victorious, come out barren: a barren triumpher, whose strength is in inertia. A man must do his own utmost: but even then, the final stroke will be delivered, or the final strength will be given from the unseen, and the man must feel it. If he doesn't feel it, he will be an inert victor, or equally inert vanquished, complacent and sterile in either case.

There must be a certain faith. And that means, an ultimate reliance on that which is beyond our will, and not contained in our ego.

We have gone to war. For a hundred years we have been piling up safety upon safety, we have grown enormously within the shell of our civilization, we have rounded off our own ego and grown almost complacent about our own triumphs of will. Till we come to a point where sex seems exhausted, and passion falls flat. When even criticism and analysis now only fatigue the mind and weary the soul.

Then we gradually, gradually formulate the desire: Oh, give us the brush with death, and let us see if we can win out all right!

We go into a war like this in order to get once more the final reduction under the touch of death. That the death is so inhuman, cold, mechanical, sordid, the giving of the body to the grip of cold, stagnant mud and stagnant water, whilst one awaits for some falling death, the knowledge of the gas clouds that may lacerate and reduce the lungs to a heaving mass, this, this sort of self-inflicted Sadism, brings almost a final satisfaction to our civilized and still passionate men.

Almost! And when it is over, and we have won out, shall we be released into a new lease of life? Or shall we only extend our dreary lease of egoism and complacency? Shall we know the barren triumph of the will?—or the equally barren triumph inertia, helplessness, barren irresponsibility.

And still, as far as there is any passion in the war, it is a passion for the embrace with death. The desire to deal death and to take death. The enemy is the bride, whose body we will reduce with rapture of agony and wounds. We are the bridegroom, engaged with him in the long, voluptuous embrace, the giving of agony, the rising and rising of the slow unwilling transport of misery, the soaking-in of day after day of wet mud, in penetration of the heavy, sordid, unendurable cold, on and on to the climax, the laceration of the blade, like a frost through the tissue, blasting it.

This is the desire and the consummation, this is the war. But at length, we shall be satisfied, at length we shall have consummation. Then the war will end. And what then?

THE CROWN

It is not really a question of victories or defeats. It is a question of fulfilment, and release from the old prison-house of a dead form. The war is one bout in the terrific, horrible labour, our civilization laboring in child-birth, and unable to bring forth.

How will it end? Will there be a release, a relaxation of the horrible walls, and a real issuing, a birth?

Or will it end in nothing, all the agony going to stiffen the old form deader, to enclose the unborn more helplessly and drearily.

It may easily be. For behind us all, in the war, stand the old and the elderly, complacent with egoism, bent on maintaining the old form. Oh, they are the monkey grinning with anxiety and anticipation, behind us, waiting for the burnt young cat to pull the chestnut out of the fire. And in the end, they will thrill with the triumph of their egoistic will, and harden harder still with vulture-like enertia, rapacious inertia.

In sex, we have plunged the quick of creation deep into the cold flux of reduction, corruption, till the quick is extinguished. In war we have plunged the whole quick of the living, sentient body into a cold, cold flux. Much has died and much will die. But if the whole quick dies, and there remain only the material, mechanical unquickened tissue, acting at the bidding of the mechanical will, and the sterile ego triumphant, then it is a poor tale, a barrenly poor tale.

[71]

THE CROWN

I have seen a soldier at the seaside who was maimed. One leg was only a small stump, with the trouser folded back on it. He was a handsome man of about thirty, finely built. His face was sun-browned, and extraordinarily beautiful, still, with a strange placidity, something like perfection, abstract, complete. He had known his consummation. It seemed he could never desire corruption or reduction again, he had had his satisfaction of death. He was become almost impersonal, a simple abstraction, all his personality loosed and undone. He was now like a babe just born, new to begin life. Yet in a sense, still-born. The newness and candour, like a flower just unloosed, was something strange and rare in him. Yet unloosed, curiously, into the light of death.

So he came forward down the pier, in the sunshine, slowly on his crutches. Behind, the sea was milk-white and vague, as if full of ghosts, and silent, except when a long white wave plunged to silence out of the smooth, milky silence of the sea, coming from very far out of the ghostly stillness.

The maimed soldier, strong and handsome, with some of the frail candour of a newly-wakened child in his face, came slowly down the pier on his crutches, looking at everybody who looked at him. He was naïve like a child, wondering. The people stared at him with a sort of fascination. So he was rather vain, rather proud, like a vain child.

THE CROWN

He did not know he was maimed, it had not entered his consciousness. His soul, so clean and new and fine, could not conceive of such a thing. He was rather vain and slightly ostentatious, not as a man with a wound, a trophy, more as a child who is conspicuous among envious elders.

The women particularly were fascinated. They could not look away from him. The strange abstraction of horror and death was so perfect in his face, like the horror of birth on a new-born infant, that they were almost hysterical. They gravitated towards him, helplessly, they could not move away from him.

They wanted him, they wanted him so badly, that they were almost beside themselves. They wanted his consummation, his perfect completeness in horror and death. They too wanted the consummation. They followed him, they made excuses to talk to him. And he, strange, abstract, glowing still from the consummation of destruction and pain and horror, like a bridegroom just come from the bride, seemed to glow before the women, to give off a strange, unearthly radiance, which was like an embrace, a most poignant embrace to their souls.

But still his eyes were looking, looking, looking for someone who was not eager for him, to know him, to devour him, like women round a perfect child. He had not realized yet what all the attention meant, which he received. He was so strong in his new birth.

And he was looking for his own kind, for the living, the new-born, round about. But he was surrounded by greedy, voracious people, like birds seeking the death in him, pecking at the death in him.

It was horrible, rather sinister, the women round the man, there on the pier stretched from the still, sunny land over the white sea, noiseless and inhuman.

The spirit of destruction is divine, when it breaks the ego and opens the soul to the wide heavens. In corruption there is divinity. Aphrodite is, on one side, the great goddess of destruction in sex, Dionysus in the spirit. Moloch and some gods of Egypt are gods also of the knowledge of death. In the soft and shiny voluptuousness of decay, in the marshy chill heat of reptiles, there is the sign of the Godhead. It is the activity of departure. And departure is the opposite equivalent of coming together; decay, corruption, destruction, breaking down is the opposite equivalent of creation. In infinite going-apart there is revealed again the pure absolute, the absolute relation: this time truly as a Ghost: the ghost of what was.

We who live, we can only live or die. And when, like the maimed soldier on the pier with the white sea behind, when we have come right back into life, and the wonder of death fades off our faces again, what then?

Shall we go on with wide, careless eyes and the

faint astonished smile waiting all our lives for the accomplished death? Waiting for death finally? And continuing the sensational reduction process? Or shall we fade into a dry empty egoism? Which will the maimed soldier do? He cannot remain as he is, clear and peaceful.

Are we really doomed, and smiling with the wonder of doom?

Even if we are, we need not say: "It is finished." It is never finished. That is one time when Jesus spoke a fatal half-truth, in his *Consummatum Est!* Death consummates nothing. It can but abruptly close the individual life. But Life itself, and even the forms men have given it, will persist and persist. There is no consummation into death. Death leaves still further deaths.

Leonardo knew this: he knew the strange endlessness of the flux of corruption. It is Mona Lisa's ironic smile. Even Michael Angelo knew it. It is in his *Leda and the Swan.* For the swan is one of the symbols of divine corruption with its reptile feet buried in the ooze and mud, its voluptuous form yielding and embracing the ooze of water, its beauty white and cold and terrifying, like the dead beauty of the moon, like the water-lily, the sacred lotus, its neck and head like the snake, it is for us a flame of the cold white fire of flux, the phosphorescence of corruption, the salt, cold burning of the sea which corrodes all it touches, coldly reduces every sun-built form to ash, to the original elements. This is the beauty of the swan, the lotus, the snake, this cold white salty fire of infinite reduction. And there was some suggestion of this in the Christ of the early Christians, the Christ who was the Fish.

So that, when Leonardo and Michael Angelo represent Leda in the embrace of the swan, they are painting mankind in the clasp of the divine flux of corruption, the singing death. Mankind *turned back*, to cold, bygone consummations.

When the swan first rose out of the marshes, it was a glory of creation. But when we turn back, to seek its consummation again, it is a fearful flower of corruption.

And corruption, like growth, is only divine when it is pure, when all is given up to it. If it be experienced as a controlled activity within an intact whole, this is vile. When the cabbage flourishes round a hollow rottenness, this is vile. When corruption goes on within the living womb, this is unthinkable. The chicken dead in the egg is an abomination. We cannot subject a divine process to a static will, not without blasphemy and loathsomeness. The static will must be subject to the process of reduction, also. For the pure absolute, the Holy Ghost, lies also in the relationship which is made manifest by the departure, the departure *ad infinitum*, of the opposing elements.

THE CROWN

Corruption will at last break down for us the deadened forms, and release us into the infinity. But the static ego, with its will-to-persist, neutralises both life and death, and utterly defies the Holy Ghost. The unpardonable sin!

It is possible for this static will, this vile rind of nothingness, to triumph for a long while over the divine relation in the flux, to assert an absolute nullity of static form.

This we do who preserve intact our complete null concept of life, as an envelope around this flux of destruction, the war. The whole concept and form of life remains absolute and static, around the gigantic but contained seething of the fight. It is the rottenness seething within the cabbage, corruption within the old, fixed body. The cabbage does not relax, the body is not broken open. The reduction is sealed and contained.

That is our attitude now. It is the attitude of the women who flutter round and peck at death in us. This is the carrion process set in, the process of obscenity, the baboon, the vulture in us.

In so far as we fight to remain ideally intact, in so far as we seek to give and to have the experience of death, so that we may remain unchanged in our whole conscious form, may preserve the static entity of our conception, around the fight, we are obscene. We are like vultures and obscene insects.

[77]

THE CROWN

We may give ourselves utterly to destruction. Then our conscious forms are destroyed along with us, and something new must arise. But we may not have corruption within ourselves as sensationalism, our skin and outer form intact. To destroy life for the preserving of a static, rigid form, a shell, a glassy envelope, this is the lugubrious activity of the men who fight to save democracy and to end all fighting. The fight itself is divine, the relation betrayed in the fight is absolute. But the glassy envelope of the established concept is only a foul nullity.

Destruction and Creation are the two relative absolutes between the opposing infinites. Life is in both. Life may even, for a while be almost entirely in one, or almost entirely in the other. The end of either oneness is death. For life is really in the two, the absolute is the pure relation, which is both.

If we have our fill of destruction, then we shall turn again to creation. We shall need to live again, and live hard, for once our great civilized form is broken, and we are at last born into the open sky, we shall have a whole new universe to grow up into, and to find relations with. The future will open its delicate, dawning æons in front of us, unfathomable.

But let us watch that we do not preserve an enveloping falsity around our destructive activity, some nullity of virtue and self-righteousness, some conceit of the "general good" and the salvation of the

[78]

world by bringing it all within our own conceived whole form. This is the utter lie and obscenity. The ego, like Humpty Dumpty, sitting for ever on the wall.

The vulture was once, perhaps, an eagle. It became a supreme strong bird, almost like the phoenix. But at a certain point, it said: "I am It." And then it proceeded to preserve its own static form crystal about the flux of corruption, fixed, absolute as a crystal, about the horrible seethe of corruption. Then the eagle became a vulture.

And the dog, through cowardice, arrested itself at a certain point and became domestic, or a hyæna, preserving a glassy, fixed form about a voracious seethe of corruption.

And the baboon, almost a man, or almost a high beast, arrested himself and became obscene, a grey, hoary rind closed upon an activity of strong corruption.

And the louse, in its little glassy envelope, brings everything into the corrupting pot of its little belly.

And these are all perfectly-arrested egoists, asserting themselves static and foul, triumphant in inertia and in will.

Let us watch that we do not turn either into carrion or into carrion eaters. Let us watch that we do not become, in the vulgar triumph of our will, and the obscene inertia of our ego, vultures who feed on putrescence. The lust for death, for pain, for torture, is even then better than this fatal triumph of inertia and the egoistic will. Anything is better than that. The Red Indians, full of Sadism and self-torture and death, destroyed themselves. But the eagle, when it gets stuck and can know no more blossoming turns into a vulture with a naked head, and becomes carrion-foul.

There must always be some balance between the passion for destruction and the passion for creation, in every living activity; for in the race to destruction we can utterly destroy the vital quick of our being, leave us amorphous, undistinguished, vegetable; and in the race for creation we can lose ourselves in mere production, and pile ourselves over with dead null monstrosities of obsolete form. All birth comes with the reduction of old tissue. But the reduction is not the birth. That is the fallacy of all of us, who represent the old tissue now. In this fallacy we go careering down the slope in our voluptuousness of death and horror, careering into oblivion, like Hippolytus trammelled up and borne away in the traces of his maddened horses.

Who says that the spirit of destruction will outrun itself? Not till the driver be annihilated. Then the destructive career will run itself out.

And then what?

But neither destruction nor production is, in itself,

evil. The danger lies in the fall into egoism, which neutralises both. When destruction and production alike are mechanical, meaningless.

The race of destruction may outrun itself. But still the form may remain intact, the old imprisoning laws. Only those who have not travelled to the confines will be left, the mean, the average, the laborers, the slaves: all of them little crowned egos.

Still the ancient mummy will have the people within its belly. There they will be slaves: not to the enemy, but to themselves, the concept established about them: being slaves, they will be happy enclosed within the tomb-like belly of a concept, like goldfish in a bowl, which think themselves the centre of the universe.

This is like the vultures of the mountains. They have kept the form and height of eagles. But their souls have turned into the souls of slaves and carrion eaters. Their size, their strength, their supremacy of the mountains, remains intact. But they have become carrion eaters.

This is the tomb, the whited sepulchre, this very form, this liberty, this ideal for which we are fighting. The Germans are fighting for another sepulchre. Theirs is the sepulchre of the Eagle become vulture, ours is the sepulchre of the lion become dog: soon to become hyæna.

But we would have our own sepulchre, in which

we shall dwell secure when the rage of destruction is over. Let it be the sepulchre of the dog or the vulture, the sepulchre of democracy or aristocracy, what does it matter! Inside it, the worms will jig the same jazzy dances, and heave and struggle to get hold of vast and vaster stores of carrion, or its equivalent, gold.

The carrion birds, aristocrats, sit up high and remote, on the sterile rocks of the old absolute, their obscene heads gripped hard and small, like knots of stone clenched upon themselves for ever. The carrion dogs and hyænas of the old, arid, democratic absolute, prowl among the bare stones of the common earth, in numbers, their loins cringing, their heads sharpened to stone.

Those who will hold power, afterwards, they will sit on their rocks and heights of unutterable morality, which have become foul through the course of ages, like vultures upon the unchangeable mountain-tops. The fixed, existing form will persist for ever beneath them, about them, they will have become the spirit incarnate of the fixed form of life. They will eat carrion, having become a static hunger for keen putrescence. This alone will support the incarnation of hoary fixity which they are. And beside the carrion they will fight the multitudes of hoary, obscene dogs, which also persist. It is the mortal form become null and fixed and enduring, glassy, horrible, beyond life and death, beyond consummation, the awful, stony nullity. It is timeless, almost as the rainbow.

But it is not utterly timeless. It is only unthinkably slow, static in its passing away, perpetuated.

Its very aspect of timelessness is a fraud.

What is evil?—not death, nor the blood-devouring Moloch, but this spirit of perpetuation and apparent timelessness, this obscenity which holds the great carrion birds, and the carrion dogs. The tiger, the hawk, the weasel, are beautiful things to me; and as they strike the dove and the hare, that is the will of God, it is a consummation, a bringing together of two extremes, a making perfect one from the duality.

But the baboon, and the hyæna, the vulture, the condor, and the carrion crow, these fill me with fear and horror. These are the highly developed life-forms, now arrested, petrified, frozen, falsely, timeless. The baboon was almost as man, the hyæna as the lion: the vulture and the condor are greater than the eagle, the carrion crow is stronger than the hawk. And these obscene beasts are not ashamed. They are stark and static, they are not mixed. Their will is hoary, ageless. Before us, the Egyptians have known them and worshipped them.

The baboon, with his intelligence and his unthinkable loins, the cunning hyæna with his cringing, stricken loins, these are the static form of one achieved ego, the egoistic Christian, the democratic, the unselfish. The vulture, with her naked neck and naked, small stony head, this is the static form of the other achieved ego, the eagle, the Self, aristocratic, lordly, pagan.

It is unthinkable and unendurable. Yet we are drawn more and more in this direction. After the supreme intelligence, the baboon, after the supreme pride, the vulture. The millionaire: the international financier: the bankers of this world. The baboons, the hyænas, the vultures.

The snake is the spirit of the great corruptive principle, the festering cold of the marsh. This is how he seems, as we look back. We revolt from him, but we share the same life and tide of life as he. He struggles as we struggle, he enjoys the sun, he comes to the water to drink, he curls up, hides himself to sleep. And under the low skies of the far past æons, he emerged a king out of chaos, a long beam of new life. But the vulture looms out in sleep like a rock, invincible within the hoary, static form, invincible against the flux of both eternities.

One day there was a loud, terrible scream from the garden, tearing the soul. Oh, and it was a snake lying on the warm garden bed, and in his teeth the leg of a frog, a frog spread out, screaming with horror. We ran near. The snake glanced at us sharply, holding fast to the frog, trying to get further hold. In so trying, it let the frog escape, which leaped convulsed, away. Then the snake slid noiselessly under cover, sullenly, never looking at us again.

We were all white with fear. But why? In the world of twilight as in the world of light, one beast shall devour another. The world of corruption has its stages, where the lower shall devour the higher, *ad infinitum*.

So a snake, also, devours the fascinated bird, the little, static bird with its tiny skull. Yet is there no great reptile that shall swallow the vulture?

As yet, the vulture is beyond life or change. It stands hard, immune within the principle of corruption, and the principle of creation, unbreakable. It is kept static by the fire of putrescence, which makes the void within balance the void without. It is a changeless tomb wherein the latter stages of corruption take place, counteracting perfectly the action of life. Life devours death to keep the static nullity of the form.

So the ragged, grey-and-black vulture sits hulked, motionless, like a hoary, foul piece of living rock, its naked head and neck sunk in, only the curved beak protruding, the naked eyelids lowered. Motionless, beyond life, it sits on the sterile heights.

It does not sleep, it stays utterly static. When it spreads its great wings and floats down the air, still it is static, still this is the sleep, a dream-floating. When it rips up carrion and swallows it, it is still

the same dream-motion, static, beyond the inglutina-
tion. The naked, obscene head is always fast locked,
like stone.

It is this naked, obscene head of a bird, sleep-
locked, a petrified knot of sleep, that I cannot bear
to think of. When I think of it, I neither live nor die,
I am petrified into foulness. The knot of volition,
the will knotted upon a perpetuated moment, will
not now be unloosed for ever. It will remain hoary,
unchanging, timeless. Till it disappears, suddenly.
Amid all the flux of time, of the two eternities, this
head remains unbroken in a cold, rivetted sleep. But
one day it will be broken.

I am set utterly against this small, naked, stone-
clinched head, it is a foul vision I want to wipe away.
But I am set utterly also against the loathsome,
cringing, imprisoned loins of the hyæna, that cringe
down the hind legs of the beast with their static
weight. Again the static will has knotted into rivetted, endless nullity, but here upon the loins. In the
vulture, the head is turned to stone, the fire is in the
talons and the beak. In the hoary, glassy hyæna,
the loins are turned to stone, heavy, sinking down
to earth, almost dragged along, the fire is in the
white eyes, and in the fangs. The hyæna can scarcely
see and hear the living world; it draws back on to
the stony fixity of its own loins, draws back upon
its own nullity, sightless save for carrion. The vul-

ture can neither see nor hear the living world, it is one supreme glance, the glance in search of carrion, its own absolute quenching, beyond which is nothing.

This is the end, and beyond the end. This is beyond the beginning and the end. Here the beginning and the end are revoked. The vulture, revoking the end, the end petrified upon the beginning, is a nullity. The hyæna, the beginning petrified beneath the end, is a nullity. This is beyond the beginning and the end, this is aristocracy gone beyond aristocracy, the I gone beyond the I; the other is democracy gone beyond democracy, the not-me surpassed upon itself.

This is the changelessness of the kingdoms of the earth, null, unthinkable.

This is the last state into which man may fall, in the triumph of will and the triumph of inertia, the state of the animated sepulchre.

VI

EHIND me there is time stretching back for ever, on to the unthinkable beginnings, infinitely. And this is eternity. Ahead of me, where I do not know, there is time stretching on infinitely, to eternity. These are the two eternities.

We cannot say, they are one and the same. They are two and utterly different. If I look at the eternity ahead, my back is towards the other eternity, this latter is forgotten, it *is* not. Which is the Christian attitude. If I look at the eternity behind, back to the source, then there is for me one eternity, one only. And this is the pagan eternity, the eternity of Pan. This is the eternity some of us are veering round to, in private life, during the past few years.

The two eternities are *not* one eternity. It is only by denying the very meaning of speech itself, that we can argue them into oneness. They are two, relative to one another.

They are only *one* in their mutual relation, which relation is timeless and absolute. The eternities are temporal and relative. But their relation is constant, absolute without mitigation.

The motion of the eternities is dual: they flow together, and they flow apart, they flow for ever towards union, they start back for ever in opposition, to flow for ever back to the issue, back into the unthinkable future, back into the unthinkable past.

We have known both directions. The Pagan, aristocratic, lordly, sensuous, has declared the Eternity of the Origin, the Christian, humble, spiritual, unselfish, democratic, has declared the Eternity of the Issue, the End. We have heard both declarations, we have seen each great ideal fulfilled, as far as is possible, at this time, on earth. And now we say: "There is no eternity, there is no infinite, there is no God, there is no immortality."

And all the time we know we are cutting off our nose to spite our face. Without God, without some sort of immortality, not necessarily life-everlasting, but without *something* absolute, we are nothing. Yet now, in our spitefulness of self- frustration, we would rather be nothing than listen to our own being.

God is not the one infinite, nor the other, our immortality is not in the original eternity, neither in the ultimate eternity. God is the utter relation between the two eternities, He is in the flowing together and the flowing apart.

This utter relation is timeless, absolute and perfect. It is in the Beginning and the End, just the same. Whether it be revealed or not, it is the same. It is the Unrevealed God: what Jesus called the Holy Ghost.

My immortality is not from the beginning, in my endless ancestry. Nor is it on ahead in life everlasting. My life comes to me from the great Creator, the Beginner. And my spirit runs towards the Comforter, the Goal far ahead. But I, what am I between?

These two halves I always am. But I am never *myself* until they are consummated into a spark of oneness, the gleam of the Holy Ghost. And in this spark is my immortality, my non-mortal being, that which is not swept away down either direction of time.

I am not immortal till I have achieved immortality. And immortality is not a question of time, of everlasting life. It is a question of consummate being. Most men die and perish away, unconsummated, unachieved. It is not easy to achieve immortality, to win a consummate being. It is supremely difficult. It means undaunted suffering and undaunted enjoyment, both. And when a man has reached his ultimate of enjoyment and his ultimate of suffering, *both*, then he knows the two eternities, then he is made absolute, like the iris, created out of the two. Then he is immortal. It is not a question of time. It is a question of being. It is not a question of submission, submitting to the divine grace: it is a question of submitting to the divine grace, in suffering and self-obliteration, and it is a question of conquering by divine grace, as the tiger leaps on the trembling deer, in utter satisfaction of the Self, in complete fulfilment of desire. The fulfilment is dual. And having known the dual fulfilment, then within the fulfilled soul is established the divine relation, the Holy Spirit dwells there, the soul has achieved immortality, it has attained to absolute being.

So the body of man is begotten and born in an ecstasy of delight and of suffering. It is a flame kindled between the opposing confluent elements of the air. It is the battle-ground and marriage-bed of the two invisible hosts. It flames up to its full strength, and is consummate, perfect, absolute, the human body. It is a revelation of God, it is the foam-burst of the two waves, it is the iris of the two eternities. It is a flame, flapping and travelling in the winds of mortality.

Then the pressure of the dark and the light relaxes, the flame sinks. We watch the slow departure, till only the wick glows. Then there is the dead body, cold, rigid, perfect in its absolute form, the revelation of the consummation of the flux, a perfect jet of foam that has fallen and is vanishing away. The two waves are fast going asunder, the snow-wreath melts, corruption's quick fire is burning in the achieved revelation.

THE CROWN

We cannot bear it, that the body should decay. We cover it up, we cannot bear it. It is the revelation of God, it is the most holy of all revealed things. And it melts into slow putrescence.

We cannot bear it. We wish above all to preserve this achieved and perfect form, this revelation of God. And despair comes over us when it passes away. "*Sic transit,*" we say, in agony.

The perfect form was not achieved in time, but in timelessness. It does not belong to today or tomorrow, or to eternity. It just *is*.

It is we who pass away, we and the whole flux of the two eternities, these pass. This is the eternal flux. But the God-quick, which is the constant within the flux, this is neither temporal nor eternal, it is truly timeless. And this perfect body was a revelation of the timeless God, timeless as He. If we, in our mortality are temporal, if we are part of the flux of the eternities then we swirl away in our living flux, the flesh decomposes and is lost.

But all the time, whether in the glad warm confluence of creation or in the cold flowing-apart of corruption, the same quick remains absolute and timeless, the revelation is in God, timeless. This alone of mortality does not belong to the passing away, this consummation, this revelation of God within the body, or within the soul. This revelation of God *is* God. But we who live, we are of the flux, we belong to the two eternities.

Only perpetuation is a sin. The perfect relation is perfect. But it is therefore timeless. And we must not think to tie a knot in Time, and thus to make the consummation temporal or eternal. The consummation is timeless, and we belong to Time, in our process of living.

Only Matter is a very slow flux, the waves ebbing slowly apart. So we engrave the beloved image on the slow, slow wave. We have the image in marble, or in pictured colour.

This is art, this transferring to a slow flux the form that was attained at the maximum of confluence between the two quick waves. This is art, the revelation of a pure, an absolute relation between the two eternities.

Matter is a slow, big wave flowing back to the Origin. And Spirit is a slow, infinite wave flowing back to the Goal, the ultimate Future. On the slow wave of matter and spirit, on marble or bronze or colour or air, and on the consciousness, we imprint a perfect revelation, and this is art: whether it reveal the relation in creation or in corruption, it is the same, it is a revelation of God: whether it be Piero della Francesca or Leonardo da Vinci, the *garçon qui pisse* or Phidias, or Christ or Rabelais. Because the revelation is imprinted on stone or granite, on the slow, last-receding wave, therefore it remains with us for a long, long time, like the sculptures of Egypt. But it is all the time slowly passing away, unhindered, in its own time.

It passes away, but it is not in any sense lost. Our souls are established upon all the revelations, upon all the timeless achieved relationships, as the seed contains a convoluted memory of all the revelation in the plant it represents. The flower is the burning of God in the bush: the flame of the Holy Ghost: the actual Presence of accomplished oneness, accomplished out of twoness. The true God is *created* every time a pure relationship, or a consummation out of twoness into oneness takes place. So that the poppy flower is God come red out of the poppy-plant. And a man, if he win to a sheer fusion in himself of all the manifold creation, a pure relation, a sheer gleam of oneness out of manyness, then this man is God created where before God was uncreate. He is the Holy Ghost in tissue of flame and flesh, whereas before, the Holy Ghost was but Ghost. It is true of a man as it is true of a dandelion or of a tiger or of a dove. Each creature, by some mystery, achieved a consummation in itself of all the wandering sky and sinking earth, and leaped into the other kingdom, where flowers are, of the gleaming Ghost. So it is for ever. The two waves of Time flow in from the eternities, towards a meeting, a consummation. And the meeting, the consummation, is heaven, is absolute. All the while, as long as time lasts, the shock of the two waves passed into oneness, there is a new heaven. All the while, heaven is created from the flux of time, the galaxies between the night. And we too may be heavenly bodies, however we swirl back in the flux. When we have surged into being, when we have caught fire with friction, we are the immortals of heaven, the invisible stars that make the galaxy of night, no matter how the skies are tossed about. We can forget, but we cannot cease to be. Life nor death makes any difference, once we *are*.

For ever the kingdom of Heaven is established more perfectly, more beautifully, between the flux of the two eternities.

One by one, in our consummation, we pass, a new star, into the galaxy that arches between the night-fall and the dawn, one by one, like the bushes in the desert, we take fire with God, and burn timelessly: and within the flame is heaven that has come to pass. Every flower that comes out, every bird that sings, every hawk that drops like a blade on her prey, every tiger flashing his paws, every serpent hissing out poison, every dove bubbling in the leaves, this is timeless heaven established from the flood, in this we have our form and our being. Every night new Heaven may ripple into being, every era a new Cycle of God may take place.

But it is all timeless. The error of errors is to try to keep heaven fixed and rocking like a boat anchored within the flux of time. Then there is sure to be shipwreck: *"Die Wellen verschlingen am Ende Schiffer und Kahn."* From the flux of time Heaven takes place in timelessness. The flux must go on.

This is sin, this tying the knot in Time, this anchoring the ark of eternal truth upon the waters. There is no ark, there is no eternal system, there is no rock of eternal truth. In Time and in Eternity all is flux. Only in the other dimension, which is not the time-space dimension, is there Heaven. We can no more *stay* in this heaven, than the flower can stay on its stem. We come and go.

So the body that came into being and walked transfigured in heavenliness must lie down and fuse away in the slow fire of corruption. Time swirls away, out of sight of the heavenliness. Heaven is not here nor there nor anywhere. Heaven is in the other dimension. In the young, in the unborn, this kingdom of Heaven which was revealed and has passed away, is established; of this Heaven the young and the unborn have their being. And if in us the Heaven be not revealed, if there be no transfiguration, no consummation, then the infants cry in the night, in want, void, strong want.

This is evil, this desire for constancy, for fixity in the temporal world. This is the denial of the absolute good, the revocation of the Kingdom of Heaven.

We cannot know God, in terms of the permanent,

temporal world; we cannot. We can only know the *revelation* of God in the physical world And the revelation of God is God. But it vanishes as the rainbow. The revelation is a condition in the whole flux of time. When this condition has passed away, the revelation is no more revealed. It has gone. And then God is gone, except to memory, a remembering of a critical moment within the flux. But there is no revelation of God in memory. Memory is not truth. Memory is persistence, perpetuation of a momentary cohesion in the flux. God is gone, until next time. But the next time will come. And then again we shall *see* God, and once more, it will be different. It is always different.

And we are all, now, living on the stale memory of a revelation of God. Which is purely a repetitive and temporal thing. But it contains us, it is our prison.

Whereas, there is nothing for a man to do but to behold God, and to become God. It is no good living on memory. When the flower opens, see him, don't remember him. When the sun shines, be him, and then cease again.

So we seek war, death, to kill this memory within us. We hate this imprisoning memory so much, we will kill the whole world rather than remain in prison to it. But why do we not create a new revelation of God, instead of seeking merely the destruction of the old revelations? We do this, because we are cowards. We say "The great revelation cannot be destroyed, but I, who am a failure, I can be destroyed". So we destroy the individual stones rather than decide to pull down the whole edifice. The edifice must stand, but the individual bricks must sacrifice themselves. So carefully we remove single lives from the edifice, and we destroy these single lives, carefully supporting the edifice in the weakened place.

And the soldier says: "I die for my God and my Country". When, as a matter of fact, in his death his God and his country are so much destroyed.

But we must always lie, always convert our action to a lie. We know that we are living in a state of falsity, that all our social and religious form is dead, a crystallised lie. Yet we say: "We will die for our social and religious form".

In truth, we proceed to die because the whole frame of our life is a falsity, and we know that, if we die sufficiently, the whole frame and form and edifice will collapse upon itself. But it were much better to pull it down and have a great clear space, than to have it collapse on top of us. For we shall be like Samson, buried among the ruins.

And moreover, if we are like Samson, trying to pull the temple down, we must remember that the next generation will be none the less slaves, sightless, in Gaza, at the mill. And they will be by no means eager to commit suicide by bringing more temple beams down with a bang on their heads. They will say: "It is a very nice temple, quite weathertight. What's wrong with it?" They will be near enough to extinction to be very canny and cautious about imperilling themselves.

No, if we are to break through, it must be in the strength of life bubbling inside us. The chicken does not break the shell out of animosity against the shell. It bursts out in its blind desire to move under a greater heavens.

And so must we. We must burst out, and move under a greater heavens. As the chicken bursts out, and has a whole new universe to get into relationship with.

Our universe is not much more than a mannerism with us now. If we break through, we shall find, that man is not man, as he seems to be, nor woman woman. The present seeming is a ridiculous travesty. And even the sun is not the sun as it appears to be. It is something tingling with magnificence.

And then starts the one glorious activity of man: the getting himself into a new relationship with a new heaven and a new earth. Oh, if we knew, the earth is everything and the sun is everything that we have missed knowing. But if we persist in our attitude of parasites on the body of earth and sun, the earth and the sun will be mere victims on which we feed our louse-like complacency for a long time yet: we, a myriad myriad little egos, five billion feeding like one.

The thing in itself! Why I never yet met a man who was anything but what he had been *told* to be. Let a man be a man-in-himself, and then he can begin to talk about the *Ding an Sich*. Men may be utterly different from the things they now seem. And then they will behold, to their astonishment, that the sun is absolutely different from the thing they now see, and that they call "sun".

THE NOVEL

THE NOVEL

SOMEBODY says the novel is doomed. Somebody else says it is the green bay tree getting greener. Everybody says something, so why shouldn't I!

Mr. Santayana sees the modern novel expiring because it is getting so thin; which means, Mr. Santayana is bored.

I am rather bored myself. It becomes harder and harder to read the *whole* of any modern novel. One reads a bit, and knows the rest; or else one doesn't want to know any more.

This is sad. But again, I don't think it's the novel's fault. Rather the novelists'.

You can put anything you like in a novel. So why do people *always* go on putting the same thing? Why is the *vol au vent* always chicken! Chicken *vol au vents* may be the rage. But who sickens first shouts first for something else.

The novel is a great discovery: far greater than Galileo's telescope or somebody else's wireless. The novel is the highest form of human expression so far attained. Why? Because it is so incapable of the absolute.

In a novel, everything is relative to everything else, if that novel is art at all. There may be didactic bits, but they aren't the novel. And the author may have a didactic "purpose" up his sleeve. Indeed most great novelists have, as Tolstoi had his Christian-socialism, and Hardy his pessimism, and Flaubert his intellectual desperation. But even a didactic purpose so wicked as Tolstoi's or Flaubert's cannot put to death the novel.

You can tell me, Flaubert had a "philosophy", not a "purpose". But what is a novelist's philosophy but a purpose on a rather higher level? And since every novelist who amounts to anything has a philosophy—even Balzac—any novel of importance has a purpose. If only the "purpose" be large enough, and not at outs with the passional inspiration.

Vronsky sinned, did he? But also the sinning was a consummation devoutly to be wished. The novel makes that obvious: in spite of old Leo Tolstoi. And the would-be-pious Prince in *Resurrection* is a muff, with his piety that nobody wants or believes in.

There you have the greatness of the novel itself. It won't *let* you tell didactic lies, and put them over. Nobody in the world is anything but delighted when Vronsky gets Anna Karénina. Then what about the sin?—Why, when you look at it, all the tragedy comes from Vronsky's and Anna's fear of *society*. The monster was social, not phallic at all. They couldn't live in the pride of their sincere passion, and spit in Mother Grundy's eye. And that, that cowardice, was the real "sin". The novel makes it obvious, and knocks all old Leo's teeth out. "As an officer I am still useful. But as a man, I am a ruin," says Vronsky —or words to that effect. Well what a skunk, collapsing as a man and a male, and remaining merely as a social instrument; an "officer", God love us!— merely because people at the opera turn backs on him! As if people's backs weren't preferable to their faces, anyhow!

And old Leo tries to make out, it was all because of the phallic sin. Old liar! Because where would any of Leo's books be, without the phallic splendour? And then to blame the column of blood, which really gave him all his life riches! The Judas! Cringe to a mangy, bloodless Society, and try to dress up that dirty old Mother Grundy in a new bonnet and face-powder of Christian-Socialism. Brothers indeed! Sons of a castrated Father!

The novel itself gives Vronsky a kick in the behind, and knocks old Leo's teeth out, and leaves us to learn.

It is such a bore that nearly all great novelists have a didactic purpose, otherwise a philosophy, directly opposite to their passional inspiration. In

their passional inspiration, they are all phallic wor-
shippers. From Balzac to Hardy, it is so. Nay, from
Apuleius to E. M. Forster. Yet all of them, when it
comes to their philosophy, or what they think-they-
are, they are all crucified Jesuses. What a bore! And
what a burden for the novel to carry!

But the novel has carried it. Several thousands of
thousands of lamentable crucifixions of self-heroes
and self-heroines. Even the silly duplicity of *Resurrection*, and the wickeder duplicity of Salammbô,
with that flayed phallic Matho, tortured upon the
Cross of a gilt Princess.

You can't fool the novel. Even with man crucified
upon a woman: his "dear cross". The novel will
show you how dear she was: dear at any price. And
it will leave you with a bad taste of disgust against
these heroes who *turn* their women into a "dear
cross", and *ask* for their own crucifixion.

You can fool pretty nearly every other medium.
You can make a poem pietistic, and still it will be a
poem. You can write *Hamlet* in drama: if you wrote
him in a novel, he'd be half comic, or a trifle suspicious: a suspicious character, like Dostoevsky's Idiot.
Somehow, you sweep the ground a bit too clear in
the poem or the drama, and you let the human Word
fly a bit too freely. Now in a novel there's always a
tom-cat, a black tom-cat that pounces on the white
dove of the Word, if the dove doesn't watch it; and

there is a banana-skin to trip on; and you know there is a water-closet on the premises. All these things help to keep the balance.

If, in Plato's *Dialogues*, somebody had suddenly stood on his head and given smooth Plato a kick in the wind, and set the whole school in an uproar, then Plato would have been put into a much truer relation to the universe. Or if, in the midst of the Timaeus, Plato had only paused to say: "And now, my dear Cleon—(or whoever it was)—I have a belly-ache, and must retreat to the privy: this too is part of the Eternal Idea of man", then we never need have fallen so low as Freud.

And if, when Jesus told the rich man to take all he had and give it to the poor, the rich man had replied: "*All right, old sport! You are poor, aren't you? Come on, I'll give you a fortune. Come on!*" Then a great deal of snivelling and mistakenness would have been spared us all, and we might never have produced a Marx and a Lenin. If only Jesus had *accepted* the fortune!

Yes, it's a pity of pities that Mathew, Mark, Luke, and John didn't write straight novels. They did write novels; but a bit crooked. The *Evangels* are wonderful novels, by authors "with a purpose." Pity there's so much Sermon-on-the-Mounting.

"Mathew, Mark, Luke, and John
Went to bed with their breeches on!"—

as every child knows. Ah, if only they'd taken them off!

Greater novels, to my mind, are the books of the Old Testament, Genesis, Exodus, Samuel, Kings, by authors whose purpose was so big, it didn't quarrel with their passionate inspiration. The purpose and the inspiration were almost one. Why, in the name of everything bad, the two ever should have got separated, is a mystery! But in the modern novel they are hopelessly divorced. When there *is* any inspiration there, to be divorced from.

This, then, is what is the matter with the modern novel. The modern novelist is possessed, hag-ridden, by such a stale old "purpose", or idea-of-himself, that his inspiration succumbs. Of course he denies having any didactic purpose at all: because a purpose is supposed to be like catarrh, something to be ashamed of. But he's got it. They've all got it: the same snivelling purpose.

They're all little Jesuses in their own eyes, and their "purpose" is to prove it. Oh Lord!—*Lord Jim! Sylvestre Bonnard! If Winter Comes! Main Street! Ulysses! Pan!* They are all pathetic or sympathetic or antipathetic little Jesuses *accomplis* or *manqués*. And there is a heroine who is always "pure", usually, nowadays, on the muck-heap! Like the Green Hatted Woman. She is all the time at the feet of Jesus, though her behaviour there may be mislead-

ing. Heaven knows what the Saviour really makes
of it: whether she's a Green Hat or a Constant Nymph
(eighteen months of constancy, and her heart failed),
or any of the rest of 'em. They are all, heroes and
heroines, novelists and she-novelists, little Jesuses
or Jesusesses. They may be wallowing in the mire:
but then didn't Jesus harrow Hell! *A la bonne heure!*

Oh, they are all novelists with an idea of themselves! Which is a "purpose", with a vengeance! For
what a weary, false, sickening idea it is nowadays!
The novel gives them away. They can't fool the novel.

Now really, it's time we left *off* insulting the novel
any further. If your purpose is to prove your own
Jesus qualifications, and the thin stream of your inspiration is "sin", then dry up, for the interest is
dead. *Life as it is!* What's the good of pretending
that the lives of a set of tuppenny Green Hats and
Constant Nymphs is Life-as-it-is, when the novel
itself proves that all it amounts to is life as it is isn't
life, but a sort of everlasting and intricate and boring
habit: of Jesus peccant and *Jesusa peccante.*

These wearisome sickening little personal novels!
After all, they aren't novels at all. In every great
novel, who is the hero all the time? Not any of the
characters, but some unnamed and nameless flame
behind them all. Just as God is the pivotal interest
in the books of the *Old Testament.* But just a trifle
too intimate, too *frère et cochon*, there. In the great

[109]

novel, the felt but unknown flame stands behind all the characters, and in their words and gestures there is a flicker of the presence. If you are *too personal, too human*, the flicker fades out, leaving you with something awfully lifelike, and as lifeless as most people are.

We have to choose between the quick and the dead. The quick is God-flame, in everything. And the dead is dead. In this room where I write, there is a little table that is dead: it doesn't even weakly exist. And there is a ridiculous little iron stove, which for some unknown reason is quick. And there is an iron wardrobe trunk, which for some still more mysterious reason is quick. And there are several books, whose mere corpus is dead, utterly dead and non-existent. And there is a sleeping cat, very quick. And a glass lamp, that, alas, is dead.

What makes the difference? *Quien sabe!* But difference there is. And I *know* it.

And the sum and source of all quickness, we will call God. And the sum and total of all deadness we may call human.

And if one tries to find out, wherein the quickness of the quick lies, it is in a certain weird relationship between that which is quick and—I don't know; perhaps all the rest of things. It seems to consist in an odd sort of fluid, changing, grotesque or beautiful relatedness. That silly iron stove somehow *belongs*.

THE NOVEL

Whereas this thin-shanked table doesn't belong. It is a mere disconnected lump, like a cut-off finger.

And now we see the great, great merits of the novel. It can't exist without being "quick". The ordinary unquick novel, even if it be a best seller, disappears into absolute nothingness, the dead burying their dead with surprising speed. For even the dead like to be tickled. But the next minute, they've forgotten both the tickling and the tickler.

Secondly, the novel contains no didactive absolute. All that is quick, and all that is said and done by the quick, is, in some way godly. So that Vronsky's taking Anna Karénina we must count godly, since it is quick. And that Prince in *Resurrection*, following the convict girl, we must count dead. The convict train is quick and alive. But that would-be-expiatory Prince is as dead as lumber.

The novel itself lays down these laws for us, and we spend our time evading them. The man in the novel must be "quick". And this means one thing, among a host of unknown meaning: it means he must have a quick relatedness to all the other things in the novel: snow, bed-bugs, sunshine, the phallus, trains, silk-hats, cats, sorrow, people, food, diphtheria, fuchsias, stars, ideas, God, tooth-paste, lightning, and toilet-paper. He must be in quick relation to all these things. What he says and does must be relative to them all.

And this is why Pierre, for example, in *War and Peace*, is more dull and less quick than Prince André. Pierre is quite nicely related to ideas, tooth-paste, God, people, foods, trains, silk-hats, sorrow, diphtheria, stars. But his relation to snow and sunshine, cats, lightning and the phallus, fuchsias and toilet-paper, is sluggish and mussy. He's not quick enough.

The really quick, Tolstoi loved to kill them off or muss them over. Like a true Bolshevist. One can't help feeling Natasha is rather mussy and unfresh, married to that Pierre.

Pierre was what we call, "so human". Which means, "so limited". Men clotting together into social masses in order to limit their individual liabilities: this is humanity. And this is Pierre. And this is Tolstoi, the philosopher with a very nauseating Christian-brotherhood idea of himself. Why limit man to a Christian-brotherhood? I myself, I could belong to the sweetest Christian-brotherhood one day, and ride after Attila with a raw beefsteak for my saddle-cloth, to see the red cock crow in flame over all Christendom, next day.

And that is man! That, really, was Tolstoi. That, even, was Lenin, God in the machine of Christian-brotherhood, that hashes men up into social sausage-meat.

Damn all absolutes. Oh damn, damn, damn all absolutes! I tell you, no absolute is going to make the lion lie down with the lamb: unless, like the limerick, the lamb is inside.

> "They returned from the ride
> With lamb Leo inside
> And a smile on the face of the tiger!
> Sing fol-di-lol-lol!
> Fol-di-lol-lol!
> Fol-di-lol-ol-di-lol-olly!"

For man, there is neither absolute nor absolution. Such things should be left to monsters like the right-angled triangle, which does only exist in the ideal consciousness. A man can't have a square on his hypotenuse, let him try as he may.

Ay! Ay! Ay!—Man handing out absolutes to man, as if we were all books of geometry with axioms, postulates and definitions in front. God with a pair of compasses! Moses with a set square! Man a geometric bifurcation, not even a radish!

Holy Moses!

"Honour thy father and thy mother!" That's awfully cute! But supposing they are not honorable? How then, Moses?

Voice of thunder from Sinai: "*Pretend to honour them!*"

"Love thy neighbour as thyself."

Alas, my neighbour happens to be mean and detestable.

THE NOVEL

Voice of the lambent Dove, cooing: "*Put it over him, that you love him.*"

Talk about the cunning of serpents! I never saw even a serpent kissing his instinctive enemy.

Pfui! I wouldn't blacken my mouth, kissing my neighbour, who, I repeat, to me is mean and detestable.

Dove, go home!

The Goat and Compasses, indeed!

Everything is relative. Every Commandment that ever issued out of the mouth of God or man, is strictly relative: adhering to the particular time, place and circumstance.

And this is the beauty of the novel; everything is true in its own relationship, and no further.

For the relatedness and interrelatedness of all things flows and changes and trembles like a stream, and like a fish in the stream the characters in the novel swim and drift and float and turn belly-up when they're dead.

So, if a character in a novel wants two wives—or three—or thirty: well, that is true of that man, at that time, in that circumstance. It may be true of other men, elsewhere and elsewhen. But to infer that all men at all times want two, three, or thirty wives; or that the novelist himself is advocating furious polygamy; is just imbecility.

It has been just as imbecile to infer that, because

Dante worshipped a remote Beatrice, every man, all men, should go worshipping remote Beatrices.

And that wouldn't have been so bad, if Dante had put the thing in its true light. Why do we slur over the actual fact that Dante had a cosy bifurcated wife in his bed, and a family of lusty little Dantinos? Petrarch, with his Laura in the distance, had *twelve* little legitimate Petrarchs of his own, between his knees. Yet all we hear is *Laura! Laura! Beatrice! Beatrice! Distance! Distance!*

What bunk! Why didn't Dante and Petrarch chant in chorus:

> Oh be my spiritual concubine
>> Beatrice!⎱
>> Laura! ⎰
>
> My old girl's got several babies that are mine,
> But *thou* be my spiritual concubine,
>> Beatrice!⎱
>> Laura! ⎰

Then there would have been an honest relation between all the bunch. Nobody grudges the gents their spiritual concubines. But keeping a wife and family—twelve children—up one's sleeve, has always been recognised as a dirty trick.

Which reveals how *immoral* the absolute is! Invariably keeping some vital fact dark! Dishonorable!

Here we come upon the third essential quality of the novel. Unlike the essay, the poem, the drama, the book of philosophy, or the scientific treatise: all of which may beg the question, when they don't downright filch it; the novel inherently is and must be:

1. Quick.
2. Interrelated in all its parts, vitally, organically.
3. Honorable.

I call Dante's *Commedia* slightly dishonorable, with never a mention of the cosy bifurcated wife, and the kids. And *War and Peace* I call downright dishonorable, with that fat, diluted Pierre for a hero, stuck up as preferable and desirable, when everybody knows that he *wasn't* attractive, even to Tolstoi.

Of course Tolstoi, being a great creative artist, was true to his characters. But being a man with a philosophy, he wasn't true to his *own character*.

Character is a curious thing. It is the flame of a man, which burns brighter or dimmer, bluer or yellower or redder, rising or sinking or flaring according to the draughts of circumstance and the changing air of life, changing itself continually, yet remaining one single, separate flame, flickering in a strange world: unless it be blown out at last by too much adversity.

If Tolstoi had looked into the flame of his own belly, he would have seen that he didn't really like the fat, fuzzy Pierre, who was a poor tool, after all. But Tolstoi was a personality even more than a character. And a personality is a self-conscious *I am:* being all that is left in us of a once-almighty Personal God. So being a personality and an almighty *I am*, Leo proceeded deliberately to lionise that Pierre, who was a domestic sort of house-dog.

Doesn't anybody call that dishonorable on Leo's part? He might just as well have been true to *himself!* But no! His self-conscious personality was superior to his own belly and knees, so he thought he'd improve on himself, by creeping inside the skin of a lamb; the doddering old lion that he was! Leo! Léon!

Secretly, Leo worshipped the human male, man as a column of rapacious and living blood. He could hardly meet three lusty, roisterous young guardsmen in the street, without crying with envy: and ten minutes later, fulminating on them black oblivion and annihilation, utmost moral thunder-bolts.

How boring, in a great man! And how boring, in a great nation like Russia, to let its old-Adam manhood be so improved upon by these reformers, who all feel themselves short of something, and therefore live by spite, that at last there's nothing left but a lot of shells of men, improving themselves steadily emptier and emptier, till they rattle with words and formulae, as if they'd swallowed the whole encyclopædia of socialism.

But wait! There is life in the Russians. Something new and strange will emerge out of their weird transmogrification into Bolshevists.

THE NOVEL

When the lion swallows the lamb, fluff and all, he usually gets a pain, and there's a rumpus. But when the lion tries to force himself down the throat of the huge and popular lamb—a nasty old sheep, really—then it's a phenomenon. Old Leo did it: wedged himself bit by bit down the throat of wooly Russia. And now out of the mouth of the bolshevist lambkin still waves an angry, mistaken, tufted leonine tail, like an agitated exclamation mark.

Meanwhile it's a deadlock.

But what a dishonorable thing for that claw-biting little Leo to do! And in his novels you see him at it. So that the papery lips of *Resurrection* whisper: "*Alas! I would have been a novel. But Leo spoiled me.*"

Count Tolstoi had that last weakness of a great man: he wanted the absolute: the absolute of love, if you like to call it that. Talk about the "last infirmity of noble minds"! It's a perfect epidemic of senility. He wanted to *be* absolute: a universal brother. Leo was too tight for Tolstoi. He wanted to puff, and puff, and puff, till he became Universal Brotherhood itself, the great gooseberry of our globe.

Then pop went Leo! And from the bits sprang up bolshevists.

It's all bunk. No man can be absolute. No man can be absolutely good or absolutely right, nor absolutely lovable, nor absolutely beloved, nor absolutely loving. Even Jesus, the paragon, was only relatively good and relatively right. Judas could take him by the nose.

No god, that men can conceive of, could possibly be absolute or absolutely right. All the gods that men ever discovered are still God: and they contradict one another and fly down one another's throats, marvellously. Yet they are *all* God: the incalculable Pan.

It is rather nice, to know what a lot of gods there are, and have been, and will be, and that they are all of them God all the while. Each of them utters an absolute: which, in the ears of all the rest of them, falls flat. This makes even eternity lively.

But man, poor man, bobbing like a cork in the stream of time, must hitch himself to some absolute star of righteousness overhead. So he throws out his line, and hooks on. Only to find, after a while, that his star is slowly falling: till it drops into the stream of time with a fizzle, and there's *another* absolute star gone out.

Then we scan the heavens afresh.

As for the babe of love, we're simply tired of changing its napkins. Put the brat down, and let it learn to run about, and manage its own little breeches.

But it's nice to think that all the gods are God all the while. And if a god only genuinely feels to you like God, then it *is* God. But if it doesn't feel quite, quite altogether like God to you, then wait awhile, and you'll hear him fizzle.

The novel knows all this, irrevocably. "My dear," it kindly says, "one God is relative to another god, until he gets into a machine; and then it's a case for the traffic cop!"

"But what am I to do!" cries the despairing novelist. "From Amon and Ra to Mrs. Eddy, from Ashtaroth and Jupiter to Annie Besant, I don't know where I am."

"Oh yes you do, my dear!" replies the novel. "You are where you are, so you needn't hitch yourself on to the skirts either of Ashtaroth or Eddy. If you meet them, say *how-do-you-do!* to them quite courteously. But don't hook on, or I shall turn you down."

"Refrain from hooking on!" says the novel.

"But be honorable among the host!" he adds.

Honour! Why, the gods are like the rainbow, all colours and shades. Since light itself is invisible, a manifestation has got to be pink or black or blue or white or yellow or vermilion, or "tinted".

You may be a theosophist, and then you will cry: *Avaunt! Thou dark-red aura! Away!!!—Oh come! Thou pale-blue or thou primrose aura, come!*

This you may cry if you are a theosophist. And if you put a theosophist in a novel, he or she may cry *avaunt!* to the heart's content.

But a theosophist cannot be a novelist, as a trumpet cannot be a regimental band. A theosophist, or a Christian, or a Holy Roller, may be *contained* in a novelist. But a novelist may not put up a fence. The wind bloweth where it listeth, and auras will be red when they want to.

As a matter of fact, only the Holy Ghost knows truly what righteousness is. And heaven only knows what the Holy Ghost is! But it sounds all right. So the Holy Ghost hovers among the flames, from the red to the blue and the black to the yellow, putting brand to brand and flame to flame, as the wind changes, and life travels in flame from the unseen to the unseen, men will never know how or why. Only travel it must, and not die down in nasty fumes.

And the honour, which the novel demands of you, is only that you shall be true to the flame that leaps in you. When that Prince in *Resurrection* so cruelly betrayed and abandoned the girl, at the beginning of her life, he betrayed and wetted on the flame of his own manhood. When, later, he bullied her with his repentant benevolence, he again betrayed and slobbered upon the flame of his waning manhood, till in the end his manhood is extinct, and he's just a lump of half-alive elderly meat.

It's the oldest Pan-mystery. God is the flame-life in all the universe; multifarious, multifarious flames, all colours and beauties and pains and sombrenesses. Whichever flame flames in your manhood, that is you, for the time being. It is your manhood, don't make water on it, says the novel. A man's manhood is to honour the flames in him, and to know that none of them is absolute: even a flame is only relative.

But see old Leo Tolstoi wetting on the flame. As if even his wet were absolute!

Sex is flame, too, the novel announces. Flame burning against every absolute, even against the phallic. For sex is so much more than phallic, and so much deeper than functional desire. The flame of sex singes your absolute, and cruelly scorches your ego. What, will you assert your ego in the universe? Wait till the flames of sex leap at you like striped tigers.

> "They returned from the ride
> With the lady inside,
> And a smile on the face of the tiger."

You will play with sex, will you! You will tickle yourself with sex as with an ice-cold drink from a soda-fountain! You will pet your best girl, will you, and spoon with her, and titillate yourself and her, and do as you like with your sex?

Wait! Only wait till the flame you have dribbled on flies back at you, later! Only wait!

Sex is a life-flame, a dark one, reserved and mostly invisible. It is a deep reserve in a man, one of the core-flames of his manhood.

What, would you play with it? Would you make it cheap and nasty!

THE NOVEL

Buy a king-cobra, and try playing with that.
Sex is even a majestic reserve in the sun.
Oh, give me the novel! Let me hear what the novel
says.
As for the novelist, he is usually a dribbling liar.

HIM WITH HIS TAIL IN HIS MOUTH

HIM WITH HIS TAIL IN HIS MOUTH

ANSWER a fool according to his folly, philosophy ditto. Solemnity is a sign of fraud. Religion and philosophy both have the same dual purpose: to get at the beginning of things, and at the goal of things. They have both decided that the serpent has got his tail in his mouth, and that the end is one with the beginning.

It seems to me time someone gave that serpent of eternity another dummy to suck.

They've all decided that the beginning of all things is the life-stream itself, energy, ether, libido, not to mention the Sanskrit joys of Purusha, Pradhana, Kala.

Having postulated the serpent of the beginning, now see all the heroes from Moses and Plato to Bergson, wrestling with him might and main, to push his tail into his mouth.

Jehovah creates man in his Own Image, according to His Own Will. If man behaves according to the ready-made Will of God, formulated in a bunch of somewhat unsavoury commandments, then lucky man will be received into the bosom of Jehovah.

Man isn't very keen. And that is Sin, original and perpetual.

Then Plato discovers how lovely the intellectual idea is: in fact, the only perfection is ideal.

But the old dragon of creation, who fathered us all, didn't have an idea in his head.

Plato was prepared. He popped the Logos into the mouth of the dragon, and the serpent of eternity was rounded off. The old dragon, ugly and venomous, wore yet the precious jewel of the Platonic idea in his head. Unable to find the dragon wholesale, modern philosophy sets up a retail shop. You can't lay salt on the old scoundrel's tail, because, of course, he's got it in his mouth, according to postulate. He doesn't seem to be sprawling in his old lair, across the heavens. In fact, he appears to have vamoosed. Perhaps, instead of being one big old boy, he is really an infinite number of little tiny boys: atoms, electrons, units of force or energy, tiny little birds all spinning with their tails in their beaks. Just the same in detail as in the gross. Nothing will come out of the egg that isn't in it. Evolution sings away at the same old song. Out of the amœba, or some such old-fashioned entity, the dragon of evolved life stretches himself enormous and more enormous, only, at last, to return each time, and put his tail into his own mouth, and be an amœba once more. The amœba, or the electron, or whatever it may lately be—the rose would be just as scentless—is the constant, from which all manifest living creation starts out, and to which it all returns.

There was a time when man was not, nor monkey, nor cow, not catfish. But the amœba (or the electron, or the atom, or whatever it is) always was and always will be.

> Boom! tiddy-ra-ta! Boom!
> Boom! tiddy-ra-ta! Boom!

How do you know? How does anyone know, what always was or wasn't? Bunk of geology, and strata, and all that, biology or evolution.

> "One, two, three four five,
> Catch a little fish alive.
> Six, seven, eight nine ten,
> I have let him go again..."

Bunk of beginnings and of ends, and heads and tails. Why does man always want to know so damned much? Or rather, so damned little? If he can't draw a ring round creation, and fasten the serpent's tail into its mouth with the padlock of one final clinching idea, then creation can go to hell, as far as man is concerned.

There is such a thing as life, or life energy. We

know, because we've got it, or had it It isn't a constant. It comes and it goes. But we *want* it.

This I think is incontestable.

More than anything else in the world, we want to have life, and life-energy abundant in us. We think if we eat yeast, vitamines and proteids, we're sure of it. We're had. We diddle ourselves for the million millionth time.

What we want is life, and life-energy inside us. Where it comes from, or what it is, we don't know, and never shall. It is the capital X of all our knowledge.

But we want it, we must have it. It is the all in all.

This we know, now, for good and all: that which is good, and moral, is that which brings into us a stronger, deeper flow of life and life-energy: evil is that which impairs the life-flow.

But man's difficulty is, that he can't have life for the asking. "He asked life of Thee, and Thou gavest it him: even length of days for ever and ever." There's a pretty motto for the tomb!

It isn't length of days for ever and ever that a man wants. It is strong life within himself, while he lives.

But how to get it? You may be as healthy as a cow, and yet have fear inside you, because your life is not enough.

We know, really, that we can't have life for the

asking, nor find it by seeking, nor get it by striving. The river flows into us from behind and below. We must turn our backs to it, and go ahead. The faster we go ahead, the stronger the river rushes into us. The moment we turn round to embrace the river of life, it ebbs away, and we see nothing but a stony fiumara.

We must go ahead.

But which way is ahead?

We don't know.

We only know that, continuing in the way we are going, the river of life flows feebler and feebler in us, and we lose all sense of vital direction. We begin to talk about vitamines. We become idiotic. We cunningly prepare our own suicide.

This is the philosophic problem: to find the way ahead.

Allons!—there is no road before us.

Plato said that ahead, ahead was the perfect Idea, gleaming in the brow of the dragon.

We have pretty well caught up with the perfect Idea, and we find it a sort of vast, white, polished tomb-stone.

If the mouth of the serpent is the open grave, into which the tail disappears, then three cheers for the Logos, and down she goes.

We children of a later Pa, know that Life is real, Life is earnest, and the Grave is not its Goal.

HIM WITH HIS TAIL IN HIS MOUTH

Let us side-step.

All goals become graves.

Every goal is a grave, when you get there.

Well, I came out of an egg-cell, like an amœba, and I go into the grave. I can't help it. It's not my fault, and it's not my business.

I don't want eternal life, nor length of days for ever and ever. Nothing so long drawn out.

I give up all that sort of stuff.

Yet while I live, I want to live. Death, no doubt, solves its own problems. Let Life solve the problem of living.

> "Teach me to live that so I may
> Rise glorious at the Judgment Day."

I have no desire to rise glorious at any Judgment Day, when the serpent finally chokes himself with his own tail.

> "Teach me to live that I may
> Go gaily on from day to day."

Nay, in all the world, I feel the life-urge weakening. It may be, there are too many people alive. I feel it is, because there is too much automatic consciousness and self-consciousness in the world.

We can't live by loving life, alone. Life is like a capricious mistress: the more you woo her the more she despises you. You have to get up and go to something more interesting. Then she'll pelt after you.

HIM WITH HIS TAIL IN HIS MOUTH

Life is the river, darkly sparkling, that enters into us from behind, when we set our faces towards the unknown. Towards some goal!!!

But there is no eternal goal. Every attempt to find an eternal goal puts the tail of the serpent into his mouth again, whereby he chokes himself in one more last gasp.

What is there then, if there is no eternal goal?

By itself, the river of life just gets nowhere. It sinks into the sand.

The river of life follows the living. If the living don't get anywhere, the river of life doesn't. The old serpent lays him down and goes into a torpor, instead of dancing at our heels and sending the life-sparks up our legs and spine, as we travel.

So we've got to get somewhere.

Is there no goal?

"Oh man! on your four legs, your two, and your three, where are you going?"—says the Sphinx.

"I'm just going to say *How-do-you-do?* to Susan," replies the man. And he passes without a scratch.

When the cock crows, he says "*How-do-you-do?*"

"*How-do-you-do Peter? How-do-you-do? old liar!*"

"*How-do-you-do, Oh Sun!*"

A challenge and a greeting.

We live in a multiple universe. I am a chick that absolutely refuses to chirp inside the monistic egg. See me walk forth, with a bit of egg-shell sticking to my tail!

HIM WITH HIS TAIL IN HIS MOUTH

When the cuckoo, the cow, and the coffee-plant chipped the Mundane Egg, at various points, they stepped out, and immediately set off in different directions. Not different directions of space and time, but different directions in creation: within the fourth dimension. The cuckoo went cuckoo-wards, the cow went cow-wise, and the coffee-plant started coffing. Three very distinct roads across the fourth dimension.

The cow was dumb, and the cuckoo too.
They went their ways, as creatures do,
Till they chanced to meet, in the Lord's green Zoo.

The bird gave a cluck, the cow gave a coo,
At the sight of each other the pair of them flew
Into tantrums, and started their hullabaloo.

They startled creation; and when they were through
Each said to the other: till I came across you
I wasn't aware of the things I could do!

Cuckoo!
Moo!
Cuckoo!

And this, I hold, is the true history of evolution. The Greeks made equilibrium their goal. Equilibrium is hardly a goal to travel towards. Yet it's something to attain. You travel in the fourth dimension, not in yards and miles, like the eternal serpent.

HIM WITH HIS TAIL IN HIS MOUTH

Equilibrium argues either a dualistic or a plural-istic universe. The Greeks, being sane, were panthe-ists and pluralists, and so am I.

Creation is a fourth dimension, and in it there are all sorts of things, gods and what-not. That brown hen, scratching with her hind leg in such common fashion, is a sort of goddess in the creative dimension. Of course, if you stay outside the fourth dimension, and try to measure creation in length, breadth and height, you've set yourself the difficult task of mea-suring up the Monad, the Mundane Egg. Which is a game, like any other. The solution is, of course (let me whisper): *put his tail in his mouth!*

Once you realise that, willy nilly, you're *inside* the Monad, you give it up. You're inside it and you always will be. Therefore, Jonah, sit still in the whale's belly, and have a look round. For you'll *never* measure the whale, since you're inside him.

And then you see it's a fourth dimension, with all sorts of gods and goddesses in it. That brown hen, who, being a Rhode Island Red, is big and stuffy like plush-upholstery, is of course, a goddess in her own rights. If I myself had to make a poem to her, I should begin:

> Oh my flat-footed plush armchair
> So commonly scratching in the yard—!

But this poem would only reveal my own limita-tions.

[135]

HIM WITH HIS TAIL IN HIS MOUTH

Because Flat-foot is the favourite of the white leg-horn cock, and he shakes the tid-bit for her with a most wooing noise, and when she lays an egg, he bristles like a double white poppy, and rushes to meet her, as she flounders down from the chicken-house, and his echo of her *I've-laid-an-egg* cackle is rich and resonant. Every pine-tree on the mountains hears him:

$$\left.\begin{array}{l}\text{She's}\\\text{I've}\end{array}\right\}\textit{laid an egg!}$$

$$\left.\begin{array}{l}\text{She's}\\\text{I've}\end{array}\right\}\textit{laid an egg!}$$

And his poem would be:

"Oh you who make me feel so good, when you sit next me on the perch
At night! (temporarily, of course!)
Oh you who make my feathers bristle with the vanity of life!
Oh you whose cackle makes my throat go off like a rocket!
Oh you who walk so slowly, and make me feel swifter
Than my boss!
Oh you who bend your head down, and move in the under
Circle, while I prance in the upper!
Oh you, come! come! come! for here is a bit of fat from
The roast veal; I am shaking it for you."

[136]

HIM WITH HIS TAIL IN HIS MOUTH

In the fourth dimension, in the creative world, we live in a pluralistic universe, full of gods and strange gods and unknown gods; a universe where that Rhode Island Red hen is a goddess in her own right and the white cock is a god indisputable, with a little red ring on his leg: which the boss put there.

Why? Why, I mean, is he a god?

Because he is something that nothing else is. Certainly he is something that I am not.

And she is something that neither he is nor I am.

When she scratches and finds a bug in the earth, she seems fairly to gobble down the monad of all monads; and when she lays, she certainly thinks she's put the Mundane Egg in the nest.

Just part of her naive nature!

As for the goal, which doesn't exist, but which we are always coming back to: well, it doesn't spatially, or temporally, or eternally exist: but in the fourth dimension, it does.

What the Greeks called equilibrium: what I call relationship. Equilibrium is just a bit mechanical. It became very mechanical with the Greeks: an intellectual nail put through it.

I don't *want* to be "good" or "righteous"—and I won't even be "virtuous", unless "vir" means a man, and "vis" means the life-river.

But I *do* want to be alive. And to be alive, I must have a goal in the *creative*, not the *spatial* universe.

HIM WITH HIS TAIL IN HIS MOUTH

I want, in the Greek sense, an equilibrium between me and the rest of the universe. That is, I want a relationship between me and the brown hen.

The Greek equilibrium took too much for granted. The Greek never asked the brown hen, nor the horse, nor the swan, if it would kindly be equilibrated with him. He took it for granted that hen and horse would be only too delighted.

You can't take it for granted. That brown hen is extraordinarily callous to my god-like presence. She doesn't even choose to know me to nod to. If I've got to strike a balance between us, I've got to work at it.

But that is what I want: that she shall nod to me, with a *"Howdy!"*—and I shall nod to her, more politely: *"How-do-you-do, Flat-foot?"* And between us there shall exist the third thing, the *connaissance*. That is the goal.

I shall not betray myself nor my own life-passion for her. When she walks into my bedroom and makes droppings in my shoes, I shall chase her with disgust, and she will flutter and squawk. And I shall not ask her to be human for my sake.

That is the mistake the Greeks made. They talked about equilibrium, and then, when they wanted to equilibrate themselves with a horse, or an ox, or an acanthus, then horse, ox, and acanthus had to become nine-tenths human, to accommodate them. Call that equilibrium?

As a matter of fact, we don't call it equilibrium, we call it anthropomorphism. And anthropomorphism is a bore. Too much anthropos makes the world a dull hole.

So Greek sculpture tends to become a bore. If it's a horse, it's an anthropomorphised horse. If it's a Praxiteles *Hermes*, it's a Hermes so Praxitelised, that it begins sugarily to bore us.

Equilibrium, in its very best sense—in the sense the Greeks *originally* meant it—stands for the strange spark that flies between two creatures, two things that are equilibrated, or in living relationship. It is a goal: to come to that state when the spark will fly from me to Flatfoot, the brown hen, and from her to me.

I shall leave off addressing her: "*Oh my flatfooted plush arm-chair!*" I realise that is only impertinent anthropomorphism on my part. She might as well address me: "*Oh my skin-flappy split pole!*" Which would be like her impudence. Skin-flappy, of course, would refer to my blue shirt and baggy cord trousers. How would *she* know I don't grow them like a loose skin!

In the early Greeks, the spark between man and man, stranger and stranger, man and woman, stranger and strangeress, was alive and vivid. Even those Doric Apollos.

In the Egyptians, the spark between man and the living universe remains alight for ever in those early, silent, motionless statues of Pharaohs. They say, it is the statue of the soul of the man. But what is the soul of a man, except *that* in him which is himself alone, suspended in immediate relationship to the sum of things? Not isolated or cut off. The Greeks began the cutting apart business. And Rodin's re-merging was only an intellectual tacking on again.

The serpent hasn't got his tail in his mouth. He is on the alert, with lifted head like a listening, sparky flower. The Egyptians knew.

But when the oldest Egyptians carve a hawk or a Sekhet-cat, or paint birds or oxen or people: and when the Assyrians carve a she-lion: and when the cave-men drew the charging bison, or the reindeer, in the caves of Altamira: or when the Hindoo paints geese or elephants or lotus in the great caves of India whose name I forget—Ajanta!—then how marvellous it is! How marvellous is the living relationship between man and his object! be it man or woman, bird, beast, flower or rock or rain: the exquisite frail moment of pure conjunction, which, in the fourth dimension, is timeless. An Egyptian hawk, a Chinese painting of a camel, an Assyrian sculpture of a lion, an African fetish idol of a woman pregnant, an Aztec rattle-snake, an early Greek Apollo, a cave-man's paintings of a Pre-historic mammoth, on and on, how perfect the timeless moments between man and the other Pan-creatures of this earth of ours!

HIM WITH HIS TAIL IN HIS MOUTH

And by the way, speaking of cave-men, how did those prognathous semi-apes of Altamira come to depict so delicately, so beautifully, a female bison charging, with swinging udder, or deer stooping feeding, or an antediluvian mammoth deep in contemplation. It is art on a pure, high level, beautiful as Plato, far, far more "civilized" than Burne Jones. Hadn't somebody better write Mr. Wells' History backwards, to prove how we've degenerated, in our stupid visionlessness, since the cave-men?

The pictures in the cave represent moments of purity which are the quick of civilization. The pure relation between the cave-man and the deer: fifty per-cent. man, and fifty per-cent. bison, or mammoth, or deer. It is not ninety-nine per-cent. man, and one per-cent. horse: as in a Raphael horse. Or hundred per-cent. fool, as when F. G. Watts sculpts a bronze horse and calls it Physical Energy.

If it is to be life, then it is fifty per-cent. me, fifty per-cent. thee: and the third thing, the spark, which springs from out of the balance, is timeless. Jesus, who saw it a bit vaguely, called it the Holy Ghost.

Between man and woman, fifty per-cent. man and fifty per-cent. woman: then the pure spark. Either this, or less than nothing.

As for ideal relationships, and pure love, you might as well start to water tin pansies with carbolic acid (which is pure enough, in the antiseptic sense) in order to get the Garden of Paradise.

BLESSED ARE THE POWERFUL

BLESSED ARE THE POWERFUL

THE reign of love is passing, and the reign of power is coming again.

The day of popular democracy is nearly done. Already we are entering the twilight, towards the night that is at hand.

Before the darkness comes, it is as well to take our directions.

It is time to enquire into the nature of power, so that we do not crassly blunder into a new era: or fall down the gulf of anarchy, in the dark, as we cross the borders.

We have a confused idea, that *will* and power are somehow identical. We think we can have a will-to-power.

A will-to-power seems to work out as bullying. And bullying is something despicable and detestable.

Tyranny, too, which seems to us the apotheosis of power, is detestable.

It comes from our mistaken idea of power. It comes from the ancient mistake, old as Moses, of confusing power with *will*. The *power* of God, and the *will* of

God, we have imagined identical. We need only think for a moment, and we can see the vastness of difference between the two.

The Jews, in Moses' time, and again particularly in the time of the Kings, came to look upon Jehovah as the apotheosis of arbitrary *will*. This is the root of a very great deal of evil; an old, old root.

Will is no more than an attribute of the ego. It is, as it were, the accelerator of the engine: or the instrument which increases the pressure. A man may have a strong will, an iron will, as we say, and yet be a stupid mechanical instrument, useful simply as an instrument, without any *power* at all.

An instrument, even an iron one, has no power. The power has to be put into it. This is true of men with iron wills, just the same.

The Jews made the mistake of deifying Will, the ethical Will of God. The Germans again made the mistake of deifying the egoistic Will of Man: the will-to-power.

There is a certain inherent stupidity in apotheosised Will, and a consequent inevitable inferiority in the devotees thereof. They all have an inferiority complex.

Because power is not in the least like Will. Power comes to us, we know not how, from beyond. Whereas our will is our own.

When a man prides himself on something that is

just in himself, part of his own ego, he falls into conceit, and conceit carries an inferiority complex as its shadow.

If a man, or a race, or a nation is to be anything at all, he must have the generosity to admit that his strength comes to him from beyond. It is not his own, self-generated. It comes as electricity comes, out of nowhere into somewhere.

It is no good trying to intellectualise about it. All attempts to argue and intellectualise merely strangle the passages of the heart. We wish to keep our hearts open. Therefore we brush aside argument and intellectual haggling.

The intellect is one of the most curious instruments of the psyche. But, like the will, it is only an instrument. And it works only under pressure of the will.

By willing and by intellectualising we have done all we can, for the time being. We only exhaust ourselves, and lose our lives—that is, our livingness, our power to live—by any further straining of the will and the intellect. It is time to take our hands off the throttle: knowing well enough what we are about, and choosing our course of action with a steady heart.

To take one's hand off the throttle is not the same as to let go the reins.

Man lives to live, and for no other reason. And

life is not mere length of days. Many people hang on, and hang on, into a corrupt old age, just because they have *not* lived, and therefore cannot let go.

We must live. And to live, life must be in us. It must come to us, the power of life, and we must not try to get a strangle-hold upon it. From beyond comes to us the life, the power to live, and we must wisely keep our hearts open.

But the life will not come *unless* we live. That is the whole point. "To him that hath shall be given." To him that hath life shall be given life: on condition, of course, that he lives.

And again, life does not mean length of days. Poor old Queen Victoria had length of days. But Emily Brontë had life. She died of it.

And again "living" doesn't mean just doing certain things: running after women, or digging a garden, or working an engine, or becoming a member of Parliament. Just because, for Lord Byron, to sleep with a "crowned head" was life itself, it doesn't follow that it will be life for *me* to sleep with a crowned head, or even a head uncrowned. Sleeping with heads is no joke, anyhow. And living won't even consist in jazzing or motoring or going to Wembley, just because most folks do it. Living consists in doing what you really, vitally want to do: what the *life* in you wants to do, not what your ego imagines you want to do. And to find out *how* the life in you wants to be lived, and to live it, is terribly difficult. Somebody has to give us a clue.

And this is the real *exercise* of power.

That settles two points. First, power is life rushing in to us. Second, the exercise of power is the setting of life in motion.

And this is very far from *Will*.

If you want a dictator, whether it is Lenin, or Mussolini, or Primo de Rivera, ask, not whether he can set money in circulation, but if he can set life in motion, by dictating to his people.

Now, although we hate to admit it, Lenin did set life a good deal in motion, for the Russian proletariat. The Russian proletariat was like a child that had been kept under too much. So it was dying to be free. It was crazy to keep house for itself.

Now, like a child, it is keeping house for itself, without Papa or Mama to interfere. And naturally it enjoys it. For the time it's a game.

But for us, English or American or French or German people, it would not be a game. We have more or less kept house for ourselves for a long time, and it's not very thrilling after years of it.

So a Lenin wouldn't do us any good. He wouldn't set any life going in us at all.

The Gallic and Latin blood isn't thrilled about keeping house, anyhow. It wants Glory, or else ʎɹoꞁƃ. Glory on horse-back, or Glory upset. If there

[149]

was any Glory to upset, either in France or Italy or Spain, then communism might flourish. But since there isn't even a spark of Glory to blow out — Alfonso! Victor Emmanuel! Poincaré!—what's the good of blowing?

So they set up a little harmless Glory in baggy trousers—Papa Mussolini—or a bit of fat, self-loving but amiable elder-brother Glory in General de Rivera: and they call it power. And the democratic world holds up its hands, and moans: *"Dictators! Tyranny!"* While the conservative world cheers loudly, and cries: *"The Man! The Man! El hombre! L'uomo! L'homme! Hooray!!!"*

Bunk!

We want life. And we want the power of life. We want to feel the power of life in ourselves.

We're sick of being soft, and amiable, and harmless. We're sick to death of even enjoying ourselves. We're a bit ashamed of our own existence. Or if we aren't we ought to be.

But what then? Shall we exclaim, in a fat voice: *"Aha! Power! Glory! Force! The Man!"*—and proceed to set up a harmless Mussolini, or a fat Rivera? Well, let us, if we want to. Only it won't make the slightest difference to our real living. Except it's probably a good thing to have the press—the newspaper press —crushed under the up-to-date rubber heel of a tyrannous but harmless dictator.

BLESSED ARE THE POWERFUL

We won't speak of poor old Hindenburg. Except, why didn't they set up his wooden statue with all the nails knocked into it, for a President? For surely they drove *something* in, with those nails!

We had a harmless dictator, in Mr. Lloyd George. Better go ahead with the Houses of Representatives, than have another shot in that direction.

Power! How can there be power in politics, when politics is money?

Money is power, they say. Is it? Money is to power what margarine is to butter: a nasty substitute.

No, power is something you've got to respect, even revere, before you can have it. It isn't bossing, or bullying, hiring a manservant or Salvationising your social inferior, issuing loud orders and getting your own way, doing your opponent down. That isn't power.

Power is *pouvoir:* to be able to.

Might: the ability to make: to bring about that which may-be.

And where are we to get Power, or Might, or Glory, or Honour, or Wisdom?

Out of Lloyd George, or Lenin, or Mussolini, or Rivera, or anything else political?

Bah! It has to be in the people, before it can come out in politics.

Do we *want* Power, Might, Glory, Honour, and Wisdom?

If we do, we'd better start to get them, each man for himself.

But if we don't, we'd better continue our lick-spittling course of being as happy, as happy as Kings.

"The world is so full of a number of things
We ought all to be happy, as happy as Kings."

Which Kings, might we ask? Better be careful! Myself I want Power. But I don't want to boss anybody.

I want Honour. But I don't see any existing nation or government that could give it me.

I want Glory. But heaven save me from mankind.

I want Might. But perhaps I've got it.

The first thing, of course, is to open one's heart to the source of Power, and Might, and Glory, and Honour. It just depends, which gates of one's heart one opens. You can open the humble gate, or the proud gate. Or you can open both, and see what comes.

Best open both, and take the responsibility. But set a guard at each gate, to keep out the liars, the snivellers, the mongrel and the greedy.

However smart we be, however rich and clever or loving or charitable or spiritual or impeccable, it doesn't help us at all. The real power comes in to us from beyond. Life enters us from behind, where we are sightless, and from below, where we do not understand.

And unless we yield to the beyond, and take our power and might and honour and glory from the unseen, from the unknown, we shall continue empty. We may have length of days. But an empty tin can lasts longer than Alexander lived.

So, anomalous as it may sound, if we want power, we must put aside our own will, and our own conceit, and *accept* power, from the beyond.

And having admitted the power from the beyond into us, we must abide by it, and not traduce it. Courage, discipline, inward isolation, these are the conditions upon which power will abide in us.

And between brave people there will be the communion of power, prior to the communion of love. The communion of power does not exclude the communion of love. It includes it. The communion of love is only a part of the greater communion of power.

Power is the supreme quality of God and man: the power to cause, the power to create, the power to make, the power to do, the power to destroy. And then, between those things which are created or made, love is the supreme binding relationship. And between those who, with a single impulse, set out passionately to destroy what must be destroyed, joy flies like electric sparks, within the communion of power.

Love is simply and purely a relationship, and in a pure relationship there can be nothing but equality; or at least equipoise.

[153]

But Power is more than a relationship. It is like electricity, it has different degrees. Men are powerful or powerless, more or less: we know not how or why. But it is so. And the communion of power will always be a communion in inequality.

In the end, as in the beginning, it is always Power that rules the world! There *must be* rule. And only Power can rule. Love cannot, should not, does not seek to. The statement that love rules the camp, the court, the grove, is a lie; and the fact that such love has to rhyme with "grove", proves it. Power rules and will always rule. Because it was Power that created us all. The act of love itself is an act of power, original as original sin. The power is given us.

As soon as there is an *act*, even in love, it is power. Love itself is purely a relationship.

But in an age that, like ours, has lost the mystery of power, and the reverence for power, a false power is substituted: the power of money. This is a power based on the force of human envy and greed, nothing more. So nations naturally become more envious and greedy every day. While individuals ooze away in a cowardice that they call love. They call it love, and peace, and charity, and benevolence, when it is mere cowardice. Collectively they are hideously greedy and envious.

True power, as distinct from the spurious power, which is merely the force of certain human vices directed and intensified by the human will: true power never belongs to us. It is given us, from the beyond.

Even the simplest form of power, physical strength, is not our own, to do as we like with. As Samson found.

But power is given differently, in varying degrees and varying kind to different people. It always was so, it always will be so. There will never be equality in power. There will always be unending inequality.

Nowadays, when the only power is the power of human greed and envy, the greatest men in the world are men like Mr. Ford, who can satisfy the modern lust, we can call it nothing else, for owning a motor-car: or men like the great financiers, who can soar on wings of greed to uncanny heights, and even can spiritualise greed.

They talk about "equal opportunity": but it is bunk, ridiculous bunk. It is the old fable of the fox asking the stork to dinner. All the food is to be served in a shallow dish, levelled to perfect equality, and you get what you can.

If you're a fox, like the born financier, you get a bellyful and more. If you're a stork, or a flamingo, or even a *man*, you have the food gobbled from under your nose, and you go comparatively empty.

Is the fox, then, or the financier, the highest animal in creation? Bah!

Humanity never bunked itself so thoroughly as

with the bunk of equality, even qualified down to "equal opportunity".

In living life, we are all born with different powers, and different degrees of power: some higher, some lower. The only thing to do is honorably to accept it, and to live in the communion of power. Is it not better to serve a man in whom power lives, than to clamour for equality with Mr. Motor-car Ford, or Mr. Shady Stinnes? Pfui! to your equality with such men! It gives me gooseflesh.

How much better it must have been, to be a colonel under Napoleon, than to be a Marshal Foch! Oh! how much better it must have been, to live in terror of Peter the Great—who was great—than to be a member of the proletariat under Comrade Lenin: or even to *be* Comrade Lenin: though even he was great-ish, far greater than any extant millionaire.

Power is beyond us. Either it is given us from the unknown, or we have not got it. And better to touch it in another, than never to know it. Better be a Russian and shoot oneself out of sheer terror of Peter the Great's displeasure, than to live like a well-to-do American, and never know the mystery of Power at all. Live in blank sterility.

For Power is the first and greatest of all mysteries. It is the mystery that is behind all our being, even behind all our existence. Even the Phallic erection is a first blind movement of power. Love is said to call the power into motion: but it is probably the reverse: that the slumbering *power* calls love into being.

Power is manifold. There is physical strength, like Samson's. There is racial power, like David's or Mahomet's. There is mental power, like that of Socrates, and ethical power, like that of Moses, and spiritual power, like Jesus' or like Buddha's, and mechanical power, like that of Stephenson, or military power, like Napoleon's, or political power, like Pitt's. These are all true manifestations of power, coming out of the unknown.

Unlike the millionaire power, which comes out of the known forces of human greed and envy.

Power puts something new into the world. It may be Edison's gramaphone, or Newton's Law or Cæsar's Rome or Jesus' Christianity, or even Attila's charred ruins and emptied spaces. Something new displaces something old, and sometimes room has to be cleared beforehand.

Then power is obvious. Power is much more obvious in its destructive than in its constructive activity. A tree falls with a crash. It grew without a sound.

Yet true destructive power is power just the same as constructive. Even Attila, the Scourge of God, who helped to scourge the Roman world out of existence, was great with power. He was the scourge of *God:* not the scourge of the League of Nations, hired and paid in cash.

BLESSED ARE THE POWERFUL

If it must be a scourge, let it be a scourge of God. But let it be power, the old divine power. The moment the divine power manifests itself, it is right: whether it be Attila or Napoleon or George Washington. But Lloyd George, and Woodrow Wilson, and Lenin, they never had the right smell. They never even roused real fear: no real passion. Whereas a manifestation of real power arouses passion, and always will.

Time it should again.

Blessed are the powerful, for theirs is the kingdom of earth.

. . . . LOVE WAS ONCE A LITTLE BOY

.... LOVE WAS ONCE A LITTLE BOY

COLLAPSE, as often as not, is the result of persisting in an old attitude towards some important relationship, which, in the course of time, has changed its nature.

Love itself is a relationship, which changes as all things change, save abstractions. If you want something really more durable than diamonds you must be content with eternal truths like "twice two are four".

Love is a relationship between things that live, holding them together in a sort of unison. There are other vital relationships. But love is this special one.

In every living thing there is the desire, for love, or for the relationship of unison with the rest of things. That a tree should desire to develop itself between the power of the sun, and the opposite pull of the earth's centre, and to balance itself between the four winds of heaven, and to unfold itself between the rain and the shine, to have roots and feelers in blue heaven and innermost earth, both, this is a manifestation of love: a knitting together of the diverse cosmos into a oneness, a tree.

At the same time, the tree must most powerfully exert itself and defend itself, to maintain its own integrity against the rest of things.

So that love, as a desire, is balanced against the opposite desire, to maintain the integrity of the individual self.

Hate is not the opposite of love. The real opposite of love is individuality.

We live in the age of individuality, we call ourselves the servants of love. That is to say, we enact a perpetual paradox.

Take the love of a man and a woman, today. As sure as you start with a case of "true love" between them, you end with a terrific struggle and conflict of the two opposing egos or individualities. It is nobody's fault: it is the inevitable result of trying to snatch an intensified individuality out of the mutual flame.

Love, as a relationship of unison, means and must mean, *to some extent*, the sinking of the individuality. Woman for centuries was expected to sink her individuality into that of her husband and family. Nowadays the tendency is to insist that a man shall sink his individuality into his job, or his business, primarily, and secondarily into his wife and family.

At the same time, education and the public voice

urges man and woman into intenser individualism. The sacrifice takes the old symbolic form of throwing a few grains of incense on the altar. A certain amount of time, labor, money, emotion are sacrificed on the altar of love, by man and woman: especially emotion. But each calculates the sacrifice. And man and woman alike, each saves his individual ego, her individual ego, intact, as far as possible, in the scrimmage of love. Most of our talk about love is cant, and bunk. The treasure of treasures to man and woman today is his own, or her own ego. And this ego, each hopes it will flourish like a salamander in the flame of love and passion. Which it well may: but for the fact that there are two salamanders in the same flame, and they fight till the flame goes out. Then they become grey cold lizards of the vulgar ego.

It is much easier, of course, when there *is* no flame. Then there is no serious fight.

You can't worship love and individuality in the same breath. Love is a mutual relationship, like a flame between wax and air. If either wax or air insists on getting its own way, or getting its own back too much, the flame goes out and the unison disappears. At the same time, if one yields itself up to the other entirely, there is a guttering mess. You have to balance love and individuality, and actually sacrifice a portion of each.

You have to have some sort of balance.

[163]

The Greeks said equilibrium. But whereas you can quite nicely balance a pound of butter against a pound of cheese, it is quite another matter to balance a rose and a ruby. Still more difficult is it to put male man in one scale and female woman in the other, and equilibrate that little pair of opposites.

Unless, of course, you abstract them. It's easy enough to balance a citizen against a citizeness, a Christian against a Christian, a spirit against a spirit, or a soul against a soul. There's a formula for each case. Liberty, Equality, Fraternity, etc., etc.

But the moment you put young Tom in one scale, and young Kate in the other: why, not God Himself has succeeded as yet in striking a nice level balance. Probably doesn't intend to, ever.

Probably it's one of the things that are most fascinating because they are *nearly* possible, yet absolutely impossible. Still, a miss is better than a mile. You can at least draw blood.

How can I equilibrate myself with my black cow Susan? I call her daily at six o'clock. And sometimes she comes. But sometimes, again, she doesn't, and I have to hunt her away among the timber. Possibly she is lying peacefully in cowy inertia, like a black Hindu statue, among the oak-scrub. Then she rises with a sighing heave. My calling was a mere nothing against the black stillness of her cowy passivity.

Or possibly she is away down in the bottom corner,

[164]

lowing *sotto voce* and blindly to some far-off, inaccessible bull. Then when I call at her, and approach, she screws round her tail and flings her sharp, elastic haunch in the air with a kick and a flick, and plunges off like a buck rabbit, or like a black demon among the pine trees, her udder swinging like a chime of bells. Or possibly the coyotes have been howling in the night along the top fence. And then I call in vain. It's a question of saddling a horse and sifting the bottom timber. And there at last the horse suddenly winces, starts: and with a certain pang of fear I too catch sight of something black and motionless and alive, and terribly silent, among the tree-trunks. It is Susan, her ears apart, standing like some spider suspended motionless by a thread, from the web of the eternal silence. The strange faculty she has, cow-given, of becoming a suspended ghost, hidden in the very crevices of the atmosphere! It is something in her *will*. It is her tarnhelm. And then, she doesn't know me. If I am afoot, she knows my voice, but not the advancing me, in a blue shirt and cord trousers. She waits, suspended by the thread, till I come close. Then she reaches forward her nose, to smell. She smells my hand: gives a little snort, exhaling her breath, with a kind of contempt, turns, and ambles up towards the homestead, perfectly assured. If I am on horse-back, although she knows the grey horse perfectly well, at the same time she *doesn't* know what it is. She waits till the wicked Azul, who is a born cow-punching pony, advances mischievously at her. Then round she swings, as if on the blast of some sudden wind, and with her ears back, her head rather down, her black back curved, up she goes, through the timber, with surprising, swimming swiftness. And the Azul, snorting with jolly mischief, dashes after her. And when she is safely in her milking place, still she watches with her great black eyes as I dismount. And she has to smell my hand before the cowy peace of being milked enters her blood. Till then, there is something *roaring* in the chaos of her universe. When her cowy peace comes, then her universe is silent, and like the sea with an even tide, without sail or smoke: nothing.

That is Susan, my black cow.

And how am I going to equilibrate myself with her? Or even, if you prefer the word, to get in harmony with her?

Equilibrium? Harmony? with that black blossom! Try it!

She doesn't even know me. If I put on a pair of white trousers, she wheels away as if the devil was on her back. I have to go behind her, talk to her, stroke her, and let her smell my hand; and smell the white trousers. She doesn't know they are trousers. She doesn't know that I am a gentleman on two feet. Not she. Something mysterious happens in her blood and her being, when she smells me and my nice white trousers.

Yet she knows me, too. She likes to linger, while one talks to her. She knows quite well she makes me mad when she swings her tail in my face. So sometimes she swings it, just on purpose: and looks at me out of the black corner of her great, pure-black eye, when I yell at her. And when I find her, away down the timber, when she is a ghost, and lost to the world, like a spider dangling in the void of chaos, then she is relieved. She comes to, out of a sort of trance, and is relieved, trotting up home with a queer, jerky cowy gladness. But she is never *really* glad, as the horses are. There is always a certain untouched chaos in her.

Where she is when she's *in* the trance, heaven only knows.

That's Susan! I have a certain relation to her. But that she and I are in equilibrium, or in harmony, I would never guarantee while the world stands. As for her individuality being in balance with mine, one can only feel the great blank of the gulf.

Yet a relationship there is. She knows my touch and she goes very still and peaceful, being milked. I, too, I know her smell and her warmth and her feel. And I share some of her cowy silence, when I milk her. There *is* a sort of relation between us. And this relation is part of the mystery of love: the individuality on each side, mine and Susan's, suspended in the relationship.

> Cow Susan by the forest's rim
> A black-eyed Susan was to him
> And nothing more—

One understands Wordsworth and the primrose and the yokel. The yokel had no relation at all—or next to none—with the primrose. Wordsworth gathered it into his own bosom and made it part of his own nature. "I, William, am also a yellow primrose blossoming on a bank." This, we must assert, is an impertinence on William's part. He ousts the primrose from its own individuality. He doesn't allow it to call its soul its own. It must be identical with *his* soul. Because, of course, by begging the question, there is but One Soul in the universe.

This is bunk. A primrose has its own peculiar primrosy identity, and all the oversouling in the world won't melt it into a Williamish oneness. Neither will the yokel's remarking: "Nay, boy, that's nothing. It's only a primrose!"—turn the primrose into nothing. The primrose will neither be assimilated nor annihilated, and Boundless Love breaks on the rock of one more flower. It has its own individuality, which it opens with lovely naïveté to sky and wind and William and yokel, bee and beetle alike. It *is* itself. But its very floweriness is a kind of communion with all things: the love unison.

In this lies the eternal absurdity of Wordsworth's
lines. His own behaviour, primrosely, was as foolish
as the yokel's.

> "A primrose by the river's brim
> A yellow primrose was to him
>   And nothing more—"

> A primrose by the river's brim
> A yellow primrose was to him
>   And a great deal more—

> A primrose by the river's brim
> Lit up its pallid yellow glim
>   Upon the floor—

> And watched old Father William trim
> His course beside the river's brim
>   And trembled sore—

> The yokel, going for a swim
> Had very nearly trod on him
>   An hour before.

> And now the poet's fingers slim
> Were reaching out to pluck at him
>   And hurt him more.

[169]

Oh gentlemen, hark to my hymn!
To be a primrose is my whim
    Upon the floor,
    And nothing more.

The sky is with me, and the dim
Earth clasps my roots. Your shadows skim
    My face once more. . . .
    Leave me therefore
    Upon the floor;
    Say *au revoir* . . . . .

Ah William! The "something more" that the primrose was to you, was yourself in the mirror. And if
the yokel actually got as far as beholding a "yellow
primrose", he got far enough.

You see it is not so easy even for a poet to equilibrate himself even with a mere primrose. He didn't
leave it with a soul of its own. It had to have his
soul. And nature had to be sweet and pure, Williamish. Sweet-Williamish at that! Anthropomorphised!
Anthropomorphism, that allows nothing to call its
soul its own, save anthropos: and only a special brand,
even of him!

Poetry can tell alluring lies, when we let our feel-
ings, or our ego, run away with us.

And we must always beware of romance: of people
who love nature, or flowers, or dogs, or babies, or

[170]

pure adventure. It means they are getting into a love-swing where everything is easy and nothing opposes their own egoism. Nature, babies, dogs are *so* lovable, because they can't answer back. The primrose, alas! couldn't pipe up and say: "Hey! Bill! get off the barrow!"

That's the best of men and women. There's bound to be a lot of back chat. You can *Lucy Gray* your woman as hard as you like, one day she's bound to come back at you: "Who are *you* when you're at home?"

A man isn't going to spread his own ego over a woman, as he has done over nature and primroses, and dogs, or horses, or babies, or "the people", or the proletariat or the poor-and-needy. The old hen takes the cock by the beard, and says: *"That's me, mind you!"*

Man is an individual, and woman is an individual. Which sounds easy.

But it's not as easy as it seems. These two individuals are as different as chalk and cheese. True, a pound of chalk weighs as much as a pound of cheese. But the proof of the pudding is in the eating, not the scales.

That is to say, you can announce that men and women should be equal and *are* equal. All right. Put them in the scales.

Alas! my wife is about twenty pounds heavier than I am.

[171]

Nothing to do but to abstract. *L'homme est né libre:* with a napkin round his little tail.

Nevertheless, I am a citizen, my wife is a citizeness: I can vote, she can vote, I can be sent to prison, she can be sent to prison, I can have a passport, she can have a passport, I can be an author, she can be an authoress. Ooray! OO-bloomin- ray!

You see, we are both British subjects. Everybody bow!

Subjects! Subjects! Subjects!

Madame is already shaking herself like a wet hen.

But yes, my dear! we are both subjects. And as subjects, we enjoy a lovely equality, liberty, my dear! Equality! Fraternity or Sorority! my dear!

Aren't you pleased?

But it's no use talking to a wet hen. That "subject" was a cold douche.

As subjects, men and women may be equal.

But as objects, it's another pair of shoes. Where, I ask you, is the equality between an arrow and a horseshoe? or a serpent and a squash-blossom? Find me the equation that equates the cock and the hen.

You can't.

As inhabitants of my backyard, as loyal subjects of my *rancho*, they, the cock and the hen, are equal. When he gets wheat, she gets wheat. When sour milk is put out, it is as much for him as for her. She is just as free to go where she likes, as he is. And if she

likes to crow at sunrise, she may. There is no law
against it. And he can lay an egg, if the fit takes him.
Absolutely nothing forbids.

Isn't that equality? If it isn't, what is?

Even then, they're two very different objects.

As equals, they are just a couple of barnyard fowls,
clucking! generalised!

But dear me, when he comes prancing up with his
red beard shaking, and his eye gleaming, and she
comes slowly pottering after, with her nose to the
ground, they're two very different objects. You never
think of equality: or of inequality, for that matter.
They're a cock and a hen, and you accept them as such.

You don't think of them as equals, or as unequals.
But you think of them *together*.

Wherein, then, lies the togetherness?

Would you call it love?

I wouldn't.

Their two egos are absolutely separate. He's a
cock, she's a hen. He never thinks of her for a moment, as if she were a cock like himself; and she
never thinks for a moment that he is a hen like herself. I never hear anything in her squawk which
would seem to say: "*Aren't I a fowl as much as you are,
you brute!*" Whereas I always hear women shrieking
at their men: "Aren't I a human being as much as
you are?"

It seems beside the point.

[173]

I always answer my spouse, with sweet reason-
ableness: "My dear, we are both British Subjects.
What can I say more, on the score of equality? You
are a British Subject as much as I am."

Curiously, she hates to have it put that way. She
wants to be a human being as much as I am. But
absolutely and honestly, I don't know what a
human-being is. Whereas I do know what a British
Subject is. It can be defined.

And I can see how a *Civis Romanum*, or a British
Subject can be free, whether it's he or she. The he-
ness or the she-ness doesn't matter. But how a *man*
can consider himself free, I don't know. Any more
than a cock-robin or a dandelion.

Imagine a dandelion suddenly hissing: "*I am free
and I will be free!*" Then wriggling on his root like a
snake with his tail pegged down!

What a horrifying sight!

So it is when a man, with two legs and a penis, a
belly and a mouth begins to shout about being free.
One wants to ask: which bit do you refer to?

There's a cock and there's the hen, and their two
egos or individualities seem to stay apart without
friction. They never coo at one another, nor hold each
other's hand. I never see her sitting on his lap and
being petted. True, sometimes he calls for her to come
and eat a titbit. And sometimes he dashes at her and
walks over her for a moment. She doesn't seem to

[174]

mind. I never hear her squawking: "*Don't you think
you can walk over me!*"

Yet she's by no means downtrodden. She's just
herself, and seems to have a good time: and she doesn't
like it if he is missing.

So there is this peculiar togetherness about them.
You can't call it love. It would be too ridiculous.

What then?

As far as I can see, it is desire. And the desire has a
fluctuating intensity, but it is always there. His desire
is always towards her, even when he has absolutely
forgotten her. And by the way she puts her feet down,
I can see she always walks in her plumes of desirableness, even when she's going broody.

The mystery about her, is her strange undying desirableness. You can see it in every step she takes. She
is desirable. And this is the breath of her life.

It is the same with Susan. The queer cowy mystery
of her is her changeless cowy desirableness. She is
far, alas, from any bull. She never even remotely
dreams of a bull, save at rare and brief periods. Yet
her whole being and motion is that of being desirable: or else fractious. It seems to unite her with the
very air, and the plants and trees. Even to the sky
and the trees and the grass and the running stream,
she is subtly, delicately and *purely* desirable, in cowy
desirability. It is her cowy mystery. Then her frac-
tiousness is the fireworks of her desirableness.

To me she is fractious, tiresome, and a faggot. Yet the subtle desirableness is in her, for me. As it is in a brown hen, or even a sow. It is like a peculiar charm: the creature's femaleness, her desirableness. It is her sex, no doubt: but so subtle as to have nothing to do with function. It is a mystery, like a delicate flame. It would be false to call it love, because love complicates the ego. The ego is always concerned in love. But in the frail, subtle desirousness of the true male, towards everything female, and the equally frail, indescribable desirability of every female for every male, lies the real clue to the equating, or the *relating*, of things which otherwise are incommensurable.

And this, this desire, is the reality which is inside love. The ego itself plays a false part in it. The individual is like a deep pool, or tarn, in the mountains, fed from beneath by unseen springs, and having no obvious inlet or outlet. The springs which feed the individual at the depths are sources of power, power from the unknown. But it is not until the stream of desire overflows and goes running downhill into the open world, that the individual has his further, secondary existence.

Now we have imagined love to be something absolute and personal. It is neither. In its essence, love is no more than the stream of clear and unmuddied, subtle desire which flows from person to person, creature to creature, thing to thing. The moment this stream of delicate but potent desire dries up, the love has dried up, and the joy of life has dried up. It's no good trying to turn on the tap. Desire is either flowing, or gone, and the love with it, and the life too.

This subtle streaming of desire is beyond the control of the ego. The ego says: "This is *my* love, to do as I like with! This is *my* desire, given me for my own pleasure."

But the ego deceives itself. The individual cannot possess the love which he himself feels. Neither should he be entirely possessed by it. Neither man nor woman should sacrifice individuality to love, nor love to individuality.

If we lose desire out of our life, we become empty vessels. But if we break our own integrity, we become a squalid mess, like a jar of honey dropped and smashed.

The individual has nothing, really, to do with love. That is, his individuality hasn't. Out of the deep silence of his individuality runs the stream of desire, into the open squash-blossom of the world. And the stream of desire may meet and mingle with the stream from a woman. But it is never *himself* that meets and mingles with *herself:* any more than two lakes, whose waters meet to make one river, in the distance, meet in themselves.

The two individuals stay apart, for ever and ever. But the two streams of desire, like the Blue Nile and the White Nile, from the mountains one and from the low hot lake the other, meet and at length mix their strange and alien waters, to make a Nilus Flux.

See then the childish mistake we have made, about love. We have *insisted* that the two individualities should "fit". We have insisted that the "love" between man and woman must be "perfect". What on earth that means, is a mystery. What would a perfect Nilus Flux be?—one that never overflowed its banks? or one that always overflowed its banks? or one that had exactly the same overflow every year, to a hair's-breadth?

My dear, it is absurd. Perfect love is an absurdity. As for casting out fear, you'd better be careful. For fear, like curses and chickens, will also come home to roost.

Perfect love, I suppose, means that a married man and woman never contradict one another, and that they both of them always feel the same thing at the same moment, and kiss one another on the strength of it. What blarney! It means, I suppose, that they are absolutely intimate: this precious intimacy that lovers insist on. They tell each other *everything:* and if she puts on chiffon knickers, he ties the strings for her: and if he blows his nose, she holds the hanky.

Pfui! Is anything so loathsome as intimacy, especially the married sort, or the sort that "lovers" indulge in!

It's a mistake and ends in disaster. Why? Because

the individualities of men and women are incommensurable, and they will no more meet than the mountains of Abyssinia will meet with Lake Victoria Nyanza. It is far more important to keep them distinct, than to join them. If they are to join, they will join in the third land where the two streams of desire meet.

Of course, as citizen and citizeness, as two persons, even as two spirits, man and woman can be equal and intimate. But this is their outer, more general or common selves. The individual man himself, and the individual woman herself, this is another pair of shoes.

It is a pity that we have insisted on putting all our eggs in one basket: calling love the basket, and ourselves the eggs. It is a pity we have insisted on being individuals only in the communistic, semi-abstract or generalised sense: as voters, money-owners, "free" men and women: free in so far as we are all alike, and individuals in so far as we are commensurable integers.

By turning ourselves into integers: every man to himself and every woman to herself a Number One; an infinite number of Number Ones; we have destroyed ourselves as desirous or desirable individuals, and broken the inward sources of our power, and flooded all mankind into one dreary marsh where the rivers of desire lie dead with everything else, except a stagnant unity.

[179]

. . . . LOVE WAS ONCE A LITTLE BOY

It is a pity of pities women have learned to think like men. Any husband will say, *"they haven't."* But they have: they've all learned to think like some other beastly man, who is not their husband. Our education goes on and on, on and on, making the sexes alike, destroying the original individuality of the blood, to substitute for it this dreary individuality of the ego, the Number One. Out of the ego streams neither Blue Nile nor White Nile. The infinite number of little human egos makes a mosquito marsh, where nothing happens except buzzing and biting, ooze and degeneration.

And they call this marsh, with its poisonous will-o-the-wisps, and its clouds of mosquitos, *democracy*, and the reign of love!!

You can have it.

I am a man, and the Mountains of Abyssinia, and my Blue Nile flows towards the desert. There should be a woman somewhere far South, like a great lake, sending forth her White Nile towards the desert, too: and the rivers will meet among the Slopes of the World, somewhere.

But alas, every woman I've ever met spends her time saying she's as good as any man, if not better, and she can beat him at his own game. So Lake Victoria Nyanza gets up on end, and declares it's the Mountains of Abyssinia, and the Mountains of Abyssinia fall flat and cry: *"You're all that, and more, my dear!"*—and between them, you're bogged.

I give it up.

But at any rate it's nice to know *what's* wrong, since wrong it is.

If we were men, if we were women, our individualities would be lone and a bit mysterious, like tarns, and fed with power, male power, female power, from underneath, invisibly. And from us the streams of desire would flow out in the eternal glimmering adventure, to meet in some unknown desert.

Mais nous avons changé tout cela.

I'll bet the yokel, even then, was more himself, and the stream of his desire was stronger and more gurgling, than William Wordsworth's. For a long time the yokel retains his own integrity, and his own real stream of desire flows from him. Once you break this, and turn him, who was a yokel, into still another Number One, an assertive newspaper-parcel of an ego, you've done it!

But don't, dear, darling reader, when I say "desire", immediately conclude that I mean a jungleful of rampaging Don Juans and raping buck niggers. When I say that a woman should be eternally desirable, *don't* say that I mean every man should want to sleep with her, the instant he sets eyes on her.

On the contrary. Don Juan was only Don Juan because he *had* no real desire. He had broken his own integrity, and was a mess to start with. No stream of desire, with a course of its own, flowed from him. He was a marsh in himself. He mashed and trampled everything up, and desired no woman, so he ran after every one of them, with an itch instead of a steady flame. And tortured by his own itch, he inflamed his itch more and more. That's Don Juan, the man who *couldn't* desire a woman. He shouldn't have tried. He should have gone into a monastery at fifteen.

As for the yokel, his little stream may have flowed out of commonplace little hills, and been ready to mingle with the streams of any easy, puddly little yokeless. But what does it matter! And men are far less promiscuous, even then, than we like to pretend. It's Don Juanery, sex-in-the-head, no real desire, which leads to profligacy or squalid promiscuity. The yokel usually met desire with desire: which is all right: and sufficiently rare to ensure the moral balance.

Desire is a living stream. If we gave free rein, or a free course, to our living flow of desire, we shouldn't go far wrong. It's quite different from giving a free rein to an itching, prurient imagination. That is our vileness.

The living stream of sexual desire itself does not, often, in any man, find its object, its confluent, the stream of desire in a woman into which it can flow. The two streams flow together, spontaneously, not often, in the life of any man or woman. Mostly, men and women alike rush into a sort of prostitution, because our idiotic civilisation has never learned to hold in reverence the true desire-stream. We force our desire from our ego: and this is deadly.

Desire itself is a pure thing, like sunshine, or fire, or rain. It is desire that makes the whole world living to me, keeps me in the flow connected. It is my flow of desire that makes me move as the birds and animals move through the sunshine and the night, in a kind of accomplished innocence, not shut outside of the natural paradise. For life is a kind of Paradise, even to my horse Azul, though he doesn't get his own way in it, by any means, and is sometimes in a real temper about it. Sometimes he even gets a bellyache, with wet alfalfa. But even the bellyache is part of the natural paradise. Not like human *ennui*.

So a man can go forth in desire, even to the primroses. But let him refrain from falling all over the poor blossom, as William did. Or trying to incorporate it in his own ego, which is a sort of lust. Nasty anthropomorphic lust.

Everything that exists, even a stone, has two sides to its nature. It fiercely maintains its own individuality, its own solidity. And it reaches forth from itself in the subtlest flow of desire.

It fiercely resists all inroads. At the same time it sinks down in the curious weight, or flow, of that desire which we call gravitation. And imperceptibly, through the course of ages, it flows into delicate combination with the air and sun and rain.

.... LOVE WAS ONCE A LITTLE BOY

At one time, men worshipped stones: symbolically, no doubt, because of their mysterious durability, their power of hardness, resistance, their strength of remaining unchanged. Yet even then, worshipping man did not rest till he had erected the stone into a pillar, a menhir, symbol of the eternal desire, as the phallus itself is but a symbol.

And we, men and women, are the same as stones: the powerful resistance and cohesiveness of our individuality is countered by the mysterious flow of desire, from us and towards us.

It is the same with the worlds, the stars, the suns. All is alive, in its own degree. And the centripetal force of spinning earth is the force of earth's individuality: and the centrifugal force is the force of desire. Earth's immense centripetal energy, almost passion, balanced against her furious centrifugal force, holds her suspended between her moon and her sun, in a dynamic equilibrium.

So instead of the Greek: *Know thyself!* we shall have to say to every man: *"Be Thyself! Be Desirous!"*—and to every woman: *"Be Thyself! Be Desirable!"*

Be Thyself! does not mean: *Assert thy ego!* It means, be true to your own integrity, as man, as woman: let your heart stay open, to receive the mysterious inflow of power from the unknown: know that the power comes to you from beyond, it is not generated by your own will: therefore all the time, be watchful, and reverential towards the mysterious coming of power into you.

Be Thyself! is the grand cry of individualism. But individualism makes the mistake of considering an individual as a fixed entity: a little windmill that spins without shifting ground or changing its own nature. And this is nonsense. When power enters us, it does not just move us mechanically. It changes us. When the unseen wind blows, it blows upon us, and through us. It carries us like a ship on a sea. And it roars to flame in us, like a draught in a fierce fire. Or like a dandelion in flower.

What is the difference between a dandelion and a windmill?

Heap on more wood!

Even the Nirvanists consider man as a fixed entity, a changeless ego, which is capable of nothing, ultimately, but remerging into the infinite. A little windmill that can turn faster and faster, till it becomes actually invisible, and nothing remains in nothingness, except a blur and a faint hum.

I am not a windmill. I am not even an ego. I am a man.

I am myself, and I remain myself only by the grave of the powers that enter me, from the unseen, and make me forever newly myself.

And I am myself, also, by the grace of the desire that flows from me and consummates me with the other unknown, the invisible, tangible creation.

[185]

The powers that enter me fluctuate and ebb. And the desire that goes forth from me waxes and wanes. Sometimes it is weak, and I am almost isolated. Sometimes it is strong, and I am almost carried away.

But supposing the cult of Individualism, Liberty, Freedom, and so forth, has landed me in the state of egoism, the state so prettily and nauseously described by Henley in his *Invictus:* which, after all, is but the yelp of a house-dog, a domesticated creature with an inferiority complex!

> "It matters not how strait the gate,
> How charged with punishment the scroll:
> I am the master of my fate!
> I am the captain of my soul!"

Are you, old boy? Then why hippety-hop?
He was a cripple at that!
As a matter of fact, it is the slave's bravado! The modern slave is he who does not receive his powers from the unseen, and give reverence, but who thinks he is his own little boss. Only a slave would take the trouble to shout: "*I am free!*" That is to say, to shout it in the face of the open heavens. In the face of men, and their institutions and prisons. Yes-yes! But in the face of the open heavens I would be ashamed to talk about freedom. I have no life, no real power, unless it will come to me. And I accomplish nothing, not even my own fulfilled existence, unless I go forth,

delicately, desirous, and find the mating of my desire;
even if it be only the sky itself, and trees, and the cow
Susan, and the inexpressible consolation of a statue
of an Egyptian Pharaoh, or the *Old Testament*, or even
three rubies. These answer my desire with fulfilment.
What bunk then to talk about being master of my
fate! when my fate depends upon these things: —
not to mention the unseen reality that sends strength,
or life into me, without which I am a gourd rattle.

The ego, the little conscious ego that I am, that
doll-like entity, that mannikin made in ridiculous
likeness of the Adam which I am: am I going to allow that that is *all of me?* And shout about it?

Of course, if I am nothing but an ego, and woman
is nothing but another ego, then there is really no
vital difference between us. Two little dolls of conscious entities, squeaking when you squeeze them.
And with a tiny bit of an extraneous appendage to
mark which is which.

"Woman is just the same as man," loudly said the
political speaker, "Save for a very little difference."

"Three cheers for the very little difference!" says
a vulgar voice from the crowd.

But that's a chestnut.

> "Quick! Sharp! On the alert!
> Let every gentleman put on his shirt!
> And be *quick* if you please!
> Let every lady put on her chemise!"

Though nowadays, a lady's chemise won't save her face.

In or out her chemise, however, doesn't make much difference to the modern woman. She's a finished-off ego, an assertive conscious entity, cut off like a doll from any mystery. And her nudity is about as interesting as a doll's. If you can *be* interested in the nudity of a doll, then jazz on, jazz on!

The same with the men. No matter how they pull their shirts off they never arrive at their own nakedness. They have none. They can only be undressed. Naked they cannot be. Without their clothes on, they are like a dismantled street-car without its advertisements: sort of public article that doesn't refer to anything.

The ego! Anthropomorphism! Love! What it works out to in the end is that even anthropos disappears, and leaves a sawdust mannikin wondrously jazzing.

"My little sisters, the birds!" says Francis of Assisi.

"*Whew!*" goes the blackbird.

"Listen to me, my little sisters, you birds!"

"*Whew!*" goes the blackbird. "I'm a cock, mister!"

Love! What's the good of woman who isn't desirable, even though she's as pretty as paint, and the waves in her hair are as permanent as the pyramids!

He buried his face in her permanent wave, and cried: "Help! Get me out!"

Individualism! Read the advertisements! "Jew-jew's hats give a man that individual touch he so much desires. No man could lack individuality in Poppem's pyjamas." Poor devil! If he was left to his own skin, where would he be!

Pop goes the weasel!

REFLECTIONS ON THE DEATH
OF A PORCUPINE

REFLECTIONS ON
THE DEATH OF A PORCUPINE

THERE are many bare places on the little pine trees, towards the top, where the porcupines have gnawed the bark away and left the white flesh showing. And some trees are dying from the top.

Everyone says, porcupines should be killed; the Indians, Mexicans, Americans all say the same.

At full moon a month ago, when I went down the long clearing in the brilliant moonlight, through the poor dry herbage a big porcupine began to waddle away from me, towards the trees and the darkness. The animal had raised all its hairs and bristles, so that by the light of the moon it seemed to have a tall, swaying, moonlit aureole arching its back as it went. That seemed curiously fearsome, as if the animal were emitting itself demon-like on the air.

It waddled very slowly, with its white spiky spoon-tail steering flat, behind the round bear-like mound of its back. It had a lumbering, beetle's, squalid motion, unpleasant. I followed it into the darkness of the timber, and there, squat like a great tick, it began scrapily to creep up a pine-trunk. It was very like a great aureoled tick, a bug, struggling up.

I stood near and watched, disliking the presence of the creature. It is a duty to kill the things. But the dislike of killing him was greater than the dislike of him. So I watched him climb.

And he watched me. When he had got nearly the height of a man, all his long hairs swaying with a bristling gleam like an aureole, he hesitated, and slithered down. Evidently he had decided, either that I was harmless, or else that it was risky to go up any further, when I could knock him off so easily with a pole. So he slithered podgily down again, and waddled away with the same bestial, stupid motion of that white-spiky repulsive spoon-tail. He was as big as a middle-sized pig: or more like a bear.

I let him go. He was repugnant. He made a certain squalor in the moonlight of the Rocky Mountains. As all savagery has a touch of squalor, that makes one a little sick at the stomach. And anyhow, it seemed almost more squalid to pick up a pine-bough and push him over, hit him and kill him.

A few days later, on a hot, motionless morning when the pine-trees put out their bristles in stealthy, hard assertion; and I was not in a good temper, because Black-eyed Susan, the cow, had disappeared into the timber, and I had had to ride hunting her, so it was nearly nine o'clock before she was milked: Madame came in suddenly out of the sunlight, saying: "I got such a shock! There are two strange dogs, and one of them has got the most awful beard, all round his nose."

She was frightened, like a child, at something unnatural.

"Beard! Porcupine quills, probably! He's been after a porcupine."

"Ah!" she cried in relief. "Very likely! Very likely!"—then with a change of tone; "Poor thing, will they hurt him?"

"They will. I wonder when he came."

"I heard dogs bark in the night."

"Did you? Why didn't you say so? I should have known Susan was hiding—"

The ranch is lonely, there is no sound in the night, save the innumerable noises of the night, that you can't put your finger on; cosmic noises in the far deeps of the sky, and of the earth.

I went out. And in the full blaze of sunlight in the field, stood two dogs, a black-and-white, and a big, bushy, rather handsome sandy-red dog, of the collie type. And sure enough, this latter did look queer and a bit horrifying, his whole muzzle set round with white spines, like some ghastly growth; like an unnatural beard.

The black-and-white dog made off as I went

through the fence. But the red dog whimpered and hesitated, and moved on hot bricks. He was fat and in good condition. I thought he might belong to some shepherds herding sheep in the forest ranges, among the mountains.

He waited while I went up to him, wagging his tail and whimpering, and ducking his head, and dancing. He daren't rub his nose with his paws any more: it hurt too much. I patted his head and looked at his nose, and he whimpered loudly.

He must have had thirty quills, or more, sticking out of his nose, all the way round: the white, ugly ends of the quills protruding an inch, sometimes more, sometimes less, from his already swollen, blood-puffed muzzle.

The porcupines here have quills only two or three inches long. But they are devilish; and a dog will die if he does not get them pulled out. Because they work further and further in, and will sometimes emerge through the skin away in some unexpected place.

Then the fun began. I got him in the yard: and he drank up the whole half-gallon of the chickens' sour milk. Then I started pulling out the quills. He was a big, bushy, handsome dog, but his nerve was gone, and every time I got a quill out, he gave a yelp. Some long quills were fairly easy. But the shorter ones, near his lips, were deep in, and hard to get hold of, and hard to pull out when you did get hold of them.

And with every one that came out, came a little spurt of blood and another yelp and writhe.

The dog wanted the quills out: but his nerve was gone. Every time he saw my hand coming to his nose, he jerked his head away. I quieted him, and stealthily managed to jerk out another quill, with the blood all over my fingers. But with every one that came out, he grew more tiresome. I tried and tried and tried to get hold of another quill, and he jerked and jerked, and writhed and whimpered, and ran under the porch floor.

It was a curiously unpleasant, nerve-trying job. The day was blazing hot. The dog came out and I struggled with him again for an hour or more. Then we blindfolded him. But either he smelled my hand approaching his nose, or some weird instinct told him. He jerked his head, this way, that way, up, down, sideways, roundwise, as one's fingers came slowly, slowly, to seize a quill.

The quills on his lips and chin were deep in, only about a quarter of an inch of white stub protruding from the swollen, blood-oozed, festering black skin. It was very difficult to jerk them out.

We let him lie for an interval, hidden in the quiet cool place under the porch floor. After half an hour, he crept out again. We got a rope round his nose, behind the bristles, and one held while the other got the stubs with the pliers. But it was too trying. If a quill came out, the dog's yelp startled every nerve. And he was frightened of the pain, it was impossible to hold his head still any longer.

After struggling for two hours, and extracting some twenty quills, I gave up. It was impossible to quiet the creature, and I had had enough. His nose on the top was clear: a punctured, puffy, blood-darkened mess; and his lips were clear. But just on his round little chin, where the few white hairs are, was still a bunch of white quills, eight or nine, deep in.

We let him go, and he dived under the porch, and there he lay invisible: save for the end of his bushy, foxy tail, which moved when we came near. Towards noon he emerged, ate up the chicken-food, and stood with that doggish look of dejection, and fear, and friendliness, and greediness, wagging his tail.

But I had had enough.

"Go home!" I said. "Go home! Go home to your master, and let him finish for you."

He would not go. So I led him across the blazing hot clearing, in the way I thought he should go. He followed a hundred yards, then stood motionless in the blazing sun. He was not going to leave the place.

And I! I simply did not want him.

So I picked up a stone. He dropped his tail, and swerved towards the house. I knew what he was going to do. He was going to dive under the porch, and there stick, haunting the place.

THE DEATH OF A PORCUPINE

I dropped my stone, and found a good stick under the cedar tree. Already in the heat was that sting-like biting of electricity, the thunder gathering in the sheer sunshine, without a cloud, and making one's whole body feel dislocated.

I could not bear to have that dog around any more. Going quietly to him, I suddenly gave him one hard hit with the stick, crying: "Go home!" He turned quickly, and the end of the stick caught him on his sore nose. With a fierce yelp, he went off like a wolf, downhill, like a flash, gone. And I stood in the field full of pangs of regret, at having hit him, unintentionally, on his sore nose.

But he was gone.

And then the present moon came, and again the night was clear. But in the interval there had been heavy thunder-rains, the ditch was running with bright water across the field, and the night, so fair, had not the terrific, mirror-like brilliancy, touched with terror, so startling bright, of the moon in the last days of June.

We were alone on the ranch. Madame went out into the clear night, just before retiring. The stream ran in a cord of silver across the field, in the straight line where I had taken the irrigation ditch. The pine tree in front of the house threw a black shadow. The mountain slope came down to the fence, wild and alert.

"Come!" said she excitedly. "There is a big porcupine drinking at the ditch. I thought at first it was
a bear."

When I got out he had gone. But among the grasses
and the coming wild sunflowers, under the moon, I
saw his greyish halo, like a pallid living bush, moving over the field, in the distance, in the moonlit
clair-obscur.

We got through the fence, and following, soon
caught him up. There he lumbered, with his white
spoon-tail spiked with bristles, steering behind almost as if he were moving backwards, and this was
his head. His long, long hairs above the quills quivering with a dim grey gleam, like a bush.

And again I disliked him.

"Should one kill him?"

She hesitated. Then with a sort of disgust:

"Yes!"

I went back to the house, and got the little twenty-
two rifle. Now never in my life had I shot at any live
thing: I never wanted to. I always felt guns very
repugnant: sinister, mean. With difficulty I had fired
once or twice at a target: but resented doing even so
much. Other people could shoot if they wanted to.
Myself, individually, it was repugnant to me even
to try.

But something slowly hardens in a man's soul.
And I knew now, it had hardened in mine. I found the

gun, and with rather trembling hands, got it loaded. Then I pulled back the trigger and followed the porcupine. It was still lumbering through the grass. Coming near, I aimed.

The trigger stuck. I pressed the little catch with a safety-pin I found in my pocket, and released the trigger. Then we followed the porcupine. He was still lumbering towards the trees. I went sideways on, stood quite near to him, and fired, in the clear-dark of the moonlight.

And as usual I aimed too high. He turned, went scuttling back whence he had come.

I got another shell in place, and followed. This time I fired full into the mound of his round back, below the glistening grey halo. He seemed to stumble on to his hidden nose, and struggled a few strides, ducking his head under like a hedgehog.

"He's not dead yet! Oh, fire again!" cried Madame.

I fired, but the gun was empty.

So I ran quickly, for a cedar pole. The porcupine was lying still, with subsiding halo. He stirred faintly. So I turned him and hit him hard over the nose; or where, in the dark, his nose should have been. And it was done. He was dead.

And in the moonlight, I looked down on the first creature I had ever shot.

"Does it seem mean?" I asked aloud, doubtful.

Again Madame hesitated. Then: "No!" she said resentfully.

And I felt she was right. Things like the porcupine, one must be able to shoot them, if they get in one's way.

One must be able to shoot. I, myself, must be able to shoot, and to kill.

For me, this is a *volta face*. I have always preferred to walk round my porcupine, rather than kill it.

Now, I know it's no good walking 'round. One must kill.

I buried him in the adobe hole. But some animal dug down and ate him; for two days later there lay the spines and bones spread out, with the long skeletons of the porcupine-hands.

The only nice thing about him—or her, for I believe it was a female, by the dugs on her belly—were the feet. They were like longish, alert black hands, paw-hands. That is why a porcupine's tracks in the snow look almost as if a child had gone by, leaving naked little human foot-prints, like a little boy.

So, he is gone: or she is gone. But there is another one, bigger and blacker-looking, among the west timber. That too is to be shot. It is part of the business of ranching: even when it's only a little half-abandoned ranch like this one.

Wherever man establishes himself, upon the earth, he has to fight for his place, against the lower orders of life. Food, the basis of existence, has to be fought for even by the most idyllic of farmers. You plant, and you protect your growing crop with a gun. Food, food, how strangely it relates man with the animal and vegetable world! How important it is! And how fierce is the fight that goes on around it.

The same when one skins a rabbit, and takes out the inside, one realises what an enormous part of the animal, comparatively, is intestinal, what a big part of him is just for food-apparatus; for *living on* other organisms.

And when one watches the horses in the big field, their noses to the ground, bite-bite-biting at the grass, and stepping absorbedly on, and bite-bite-biting without ever lifting their noses, cropping off the grass, the young shoots of alfalfa, the dandelions, with a blind, relentless, unwearied persistence, one's whole life pauses. One suddenly realises again how all creatures devour, and *must* devour the lower forms of life.

So Susan, swinging across the field, snatches off the tops of the little wild sunflowers as if she were mowing. And down they go, down her black throat. And when she stands in her cowy oblivion chewing her cud, with her lower jaw swinging peacefully, and I am milking her, suddenly the camomiley smell of her breath, as she glances round with glaring, smoke-blue eyes, makes me realise it is the sunflowers that are her ball of cud. Sunflowers! And they will go to making her glistening black hide, and the thick cream on her milk.

THE DEATH OF A PORCUPINE

And the chickens, when they see a great black beetle, that the Mexicans call a *toro*, floating past, they are after it in a rush. And if it settles, instantly the brown hen stabs it with her beak. It is a great beetle two or three inches long: but in a second it is in the crop of the chicken. Gone!

And Timsy, the cat, as she spies on the chipmunks, crouches in another sort of oblivion, soft, and still. The chipmunks come to drink the milk from the chickens' bowl. Two of them met at the bowl. They were little squirrely things with stripes down their backs. They sat up in front of one another, lifting their inquisitive little noses and humping their backs. Then each put its two little hands on the other's shoulders, they reared up, gazing into each other's faces; and finally they put their two little noses together, in a sort of kiss.

But Miss Timsy can't stand this. In a soft, white-and-yellow leap she is after them. They skip with the darting jerk of chipmunks, to the wood-heap, and with one soft, high-leaping sideways bound Timsy goes through the air. Her snow-flake of a paw comes down on one of the chipmunks. She looks at it for a second. It squirms. Swiftly and triumphantly she puts her two flowery little white paws on it, legs straight out in front of her, back arched, gazing concentratedly yet whimsically. Chipmunk does not stir. She takes it softly in her mouth, where it dangles softly, like a lady's tippet. And with a proud, prancing motion the Timsy sets off towards the house, her white little feet hardly touching the ground.

But she gets shooed away. We refuse to loan her the sitting-room any more, for her gladiatorial displays. If the chippy must be "butchered to make a Timsy holiday", it shall be outside. Disappointed, but still high-stepping, the Timsy sets off towards the clay oven by the shed.

There she lays the chippy gently down, and soft as a little white cloud lays one small paw on its striped back. Chippy does not move. Soft as thistle-down she raises her paw a tiny, tiny bit, to release him.

And all of a sudden, with an elastic jerk, he darts from under the white release of her paw. And instantly, she is up in the air and down she comes on him, with the forward-thrusting bolts of her white paws. Both creatures are motionless.

Then she takes him softly in her mouth again, and looks round, to see if she can slip into the house. She cannot. So she trots towards the wood-pile.

It is a game, and it is pretty. Chippy escapes into the wood-pile, and she softly, softly reconnoitres among the faggots.

Of all the animals, there is no denying it, the Timsy is the most pretty, the most fine. It is not her mere *corpus* that is beautiful; it is her bloom of aliveness. Her "infinite variety"; the soft, snow-flakey lightness of her, and at the same time her lean, heavy ferocity. I had never realised the latter, till I was lying in bed one day moving my toe, unconsciously, under the bedclothes. Suddenly a terrific blow struck my foot. The Timsy had sprung out of nowhere, with a hurling, steely force, thud upon the bedclothes where the toe was moving. It was as if someone had aimed a sudden blow, vindictive and unerring.

"Timsy!"

She looked at me with the vacant, feline glare of her hunting eyes. It is not even ferocity. It is the dilation of the strange, vacant arrogance of power. The power is in her.

And so it is. Life moves in circles of power and of vividness, and each circle of life only maintains its orbit upon the subjection of some lower circle. If the lower cycles of life are not *mastered*, there can be no higher cycle.

In nature, one creature devours another, and this is an essential part of all existence and of all being. It is not something to lament over, nor something to try to reform. The Buddhist who refuses to take life is really ridiculous, since if he eats only two grains of rice per day, it is two grains of life. We did not make creation, *we* are not the authors of the universe. And if we see that the whole of creation is established upon the fact that one life devours another life, one cycle of existence can only come into existence through the subjugating of another cycle of existence, then what is the good of trying to pretend that it is not so? The only thing to do is to realise what is higher, and what is lower, in the cycles of existence.

It is nonsense to declare that there *is* no higher and lower. We know full well that the dandelion belongs to a higher cycle of existence than the hartstongue fern, that the ant's is a higher form of existence than the dandelion's, that the thrush is higher than the ant, that Timsy the cat, is higher than the thrush, and that I, a man, am higher than Timsy.

What do we mean by higher? Strictly, we mean more alive. More vividly alive. The ant is more vividly alive than the pine-tree. We know it, there is no trying to refute it. It is all very well saying that they are both alive in two different ways, and therefore they are incomparable, incommensurable. This is also true.

But one truth does not displace another. Even apparently contradictory truths do not displace one another. Logic is far too coarse to make the subtle distinctions life demands.

Truly, it is futile to compare an ant with a great pine-tree, in the absolute. Yet as far as *existence* is concerned, they are not only placed in comparison to one another, they are occasionally pitted against one another. And if it comes to a contest, the little ant will devour the life of the huge tree. If it comes to a contest.

And, in the cycles of *existenc*, this is the test. From the lowest form of existence, to the highest, the test question is: *Can thy neighbour finally overcome thee?*

If he can, then he belongs to a higher cycle of existence.

This is the truth behind the survival of the fittest. Every cycle of existence is established upon the overcoming of the lower cycles of existence. The real question is, wherein does *fitness* lie? Fitness for what? Fit merely to survive? That which is only fit to survive will survive only to supply food or contribute in some way to the existence of a higher form of life, which is able to do more than survive, which can really *vive*, live.

Life is more vivid in the dandelion than in the green fern, or than in a palm tree.

Life is more vivid in a snake than in a butterfly.

Life is more vivid in a wren than in an alligator.

Life is more vivid in a cat than in an ostrich.

Life is more vivid in the Mexican who drives the wagon, than in the two horses in the wagon.

Life is more vivid in me, than in the Mexican who drives the wagon for me.

We are speaking in terms of *existence:* that is, in terms of species, race, or type.

The dandelion can take hold of the land, the palm tree is driven into a corner, with the fern.

THE DEATH OF A PORCUPINE

The snake can devour the fiercest insect.

The fierce bird can destroy the greatest reptile.

The great cat can destroy the greatest bird.

The man can destroy the horse, or any animal.

One race of man can subjugate and rule another race.

All this in terms of *existence*. As far as existence goes, that life-species is the highest which can devour, or destroy, or subjugate every other life-species against which it is pitted in contest.

This is a law. There is no escaping this law. Anyone, or any race, trying to escape it, will fall a victim: will fall into subjugation.

But let us insist and insist again, we are talking now of existence, of species, of types, of races, of nations, not of single individuals, nor of *beings*. The dandelion in full flower, a little sun bristling with sun-rays on the green earth, is a nonpareil, a nonsuch. Foolish, foolish, foolish to compare it to anything else on earth. It is itself incomparable and unique.

But that is the fourth dimension, of *being*. It is in the fourth dimension, nowhere else.

Because, in the time-space dimension, any man may tread on the yellow sun-mirror, and it is gone. Any cow may swallow it. Any bunch of ants may annihilate it.

This brings us to the inexorable law of life.

THE DEATH OF A PORCUPINE

1. Any creature that attains to its own fullness of being, its own *living* self, becomes unique, a nonpareil. It has its place in the fourth dimension, the heaven of existence, and there it is perfect, it is beyond comparison.

2. At the same time, every creature exists in time and space. And in time and space it exists relatively to all other existence, and can never be absolved. Its existence impinges on other existences, and is itself impinged upon. And in the struggle for existence, if an effort on the part of any one type or species or order of life, can finally destroy the other species, then the destroyer is of a more vital cycle of existence than the one destroyed. (When speaking of existence we always speak in types, species, not individuals. Species exist. But even an individual dandelion has *being*.)

3. The force which we call *vitality*, and which is the determining factor in the struggle for existence, is, however, derived also from the fourth dimension. That is to say, the ultimate source of all vitality is in that other dimension, or region, where the dandelion blooms, and which men have called heaven, and which now they call the fourth dimension: which is only a way of saying that it is not to be reckoned in terms of space and time.

4. The primary way, in our existence, to get vitality, is to absorb it from living creatures lower than our-

selves. It is thus transformed into a new and higher creation. (There are many ways of absorbing: devouring food is one way, love is often another. The best way is a pure relationship, which includes the *being* on each side, and which allows the transfer to take place in a living flow, enhancing the life in both beings.)

5. No creature is fully itself till it is, like the dandelion, opened in the bloom of pure relationship to the sun, the entire living cosmos.

So we still find ourselves in the tangle of existence and being, a tangle which man has never been able to get out of, except by sacrificing the one to the other.

Sacrifice is useless.

The clue to all existence is being. But you can't have being without existence, any more than you can have the dandelion flower without the leaves and the long tap root.

Being is *not* ideal, as Plato would have it: nor spiritual. It is a transcendant form of existence, and as much material as existence is. Only the matter suddenly enters the fourth dimension.

All existence is dual, and surging towards a consummation into being. In the seed of the dandelion, as it floats with its little umbrella of hairs, sits the Holy Ghost in tiny compass. The Holy Ghost is that which holds the light and the dark, the day and the night, the wet and the sunny, united in one little clue. There it sits, in the seed of the dandelion.

THE DEATH OF A PORCUPINE

The seed falls to earth. The Holy Ghost rouses, saying: *"Come!"* And out of the sky come the rays of the sun, and out of earth comes dampness and dark and the death-stuff. They are called in, like those bidden to a feast. The sun sits down at the hearth, inside the seed; and the dark, damp death-returner sits on the opposite side, with the host between. And the host says to them: *"Come! Be merry together!"* So the sun looks with desirous curiosity on the dark face of the earth, and the dark damp one looks with wonder on the bright face of the other, who comes from the sun. And the host says: *"Here you are at home! Lift me up, between you, that I may cease to be a Ghost. For it longs me to look out, it longs me to dance with the dancers."*

So the sun in the seed, and the earthy one in the seed take hands, and laugh, and begin to dance. And their dancing is like a fire kindled, a bonfire with leaping flame. And the treading of their feet is like the running of little streams, down into the earth. So from the dance of the sun-in-the-seed with the earthy death-returner, green little flames of leaves shoot up, and hard little trickles of roots strike down. And the host laughs, and says: *"I am being lifted up! Dance harder! Oh wrestle, you two, like wonderful wrestlers, neither of which can win."* So sun-in-the-seed and the death-returner, who is earthy, dance faster and faster and the leaves rising greener begin to dance in a ring above-ground, fiercely overwhelming any outsider, in a whirl of swords and lions' teeth. And the earthy one wrestles, wrestles with the sun-in-the-seed, so the long roots reach down like arms of a fighter gripping the power of earth, and strangles all intruders, strangling any intruder mercilessly. Till the two fall in one strange embrace, and from the centre the long flower-stem lifts like a phallus, budded with a bud. And out of the bud the voice of the Holy Ghost is heard crying: *"I am lifted up! Lo! I am lifted up! I am here!"* So the bud opens, and there is the flower poised in the very middle of the universe, with a ring of green swords below, to guard it, and the octopus, arms deep in earth, drinking and threatening. So the Holy Ghost, being a dandelion flower, looks round, and says: *"Lo! I am yellow! I believe the sun has lent me his body! Lo! I am sappy with golden, bitter blood! I believe death out of the damp black earth has lent me his blood! I am incarnate! I like my incarnation! But this is not all. I will keep this incarnation. It is good! But oh! if I can win to another incarnation, who knows how wonderful it will be! This one will have to give place. This one can help to create the next."*

So the Holy Ghost leaves the clue of himself behind, in the seed, and wanders forth in the comparative chaos of our universe, seeking another incarnation.

And this will go on for ever. Man, as yet, is less than half grown. Even his flower-stem has not appeared yet. He is all leaves and roots, without any clue put forth. No sign of bud anywhere.

THE DEATH OF A PORCUPINE

Either he will have to start budding, or he will be forsaken of the Holy Ghost: abandoned as a failure in creation, as the ichthyosaurus was abandoned. Being abandoned means losing his vitality. The sun and the earth-dark will cease rushing together in him. Already it is ceasing. To men, the sun is becoming stale, and the earth sterile. But the sun itself will never become stale, nor the earth barren. It is only that the *clue* is missing inside men. They are like flowerless, seedless fat cabbages, nothing inside.

Vitality depends upon the clue of the Holy Ghost inside a creature, a man, a nation, a race. When the clue goes, the vitality goes. And the Holy Ghost seeks for ever a new incarnation, and subordinates the old to the new. You will know that any creature or race is still alive with the Holy Ghost, when it can subordinate the lower creatures or races, and assimilate them into a new incarnation.

No man, or creature, or race can have vivid vitality unless it be moving towards a blossoming: and the most powerful is that which moves towards the as-yet-unknown blossom.

Blossoming means the establishing of a pure, *new* relationship with all the cosmos. This is the state of heaven. And it is the state of a flower, a cobra, a jenny-wren in spring, a man when he knows himself royal and crowned with the sun, with his feet gripping the core of the earth.

[214]

THE DEATH OF A PORCUPINE

This too is the fourth dimension: this state, this mysterious other reality of things in a perfected relationship. It is into this perfected relationship that every straight line curves, as if to some core, passing out of the time-space dimension.

But any man, creature, or race moving towards blossoming will have to draw immense supplies of vitality from men, or creatures below, passionate strength. And he will have to accomplish a perfected relation with all things.

There will be conquest, always. But the aim of conquest is a perfect relation of conquerors with conquered, for a new blossoming. Freedom is illusory. Sacrifice is illusory. Almightyness is illusory. Freedom, sacrifice, almightyness, these are all human side-tracks, cul-de-sacs, bunk. All that is real is the overwhelmingness of a new inspirational command, a new relationship with all things.

Heaven is always there. No achieved consummation is lost. Procreation goes on for ever, to support the achieved revelation. But the torch of revelation itself is handed on. And this is all important.

Everything living wants to procreate more living things.

But more important than this is the fact that every revelation is a torch held out, to kindle new revelations. As the dandelion holds out the sun to me, saying: *"Can you take it!"*

THE DEATH OF A PORCUPINE

Every gleam of heaven that is shown—like a dandelion flower, or a green beetle—quivers with strange passion to kindle a new gleam, never yet beheld. This is not self-sacrifice: it is self-contribution: in which the highest happiness lies.

The torch of existence is handed on, in the womb of procreation.

And the torch of revelation is handed on, by every living thing, from the protococcus to a brave man or a beautiful woman, handed to whomsoever can take it. He who can take it, has power beyond all the rest.

The cycle of procreation exists purely for the keeping alight of the torch of perfection, in any species: the torch being the dandelion in blossom, the tree in full leaf, the peacock in all his plumage, the cobra in all his colour, the frog at full leap, woman in all the mystery of her fathomless desirableness, man in the fulness of his power: every creature become its pure self.

One cycle of perfection urges to kindle another cycle, as yet unknown.

And with the kindling from the torch of revelation comes the inrush of vitality, and the need to consume and *consummate* the lower cycles of existence, into a new thing. This consuming and this consummating means conquest, and fearless mastery. Freedom lies in the honourable yielding towards the new flame, and the honourable mastery of that which shall be new, over that which must yield. As I must master my horses, which are in a lower cycle of existence. And they, they are relieved and *happy* to serve. If I turn them loose into the mountain ranges, to run wild till they die, the thrill of real happiness is gone out of their lives.

Every lower order seeks in some measure to serve a higher order: and rebels against being conquered.

It is always conquest, and it always will be conquest. If the conquered be an old, declining race, they will have handed on their torch to the conqueror: who will burn his fingers badly, if he is too flippant. And if the conquered be a barbaric race, they will consume the fire of the conqueror, and leave him flameless, unless he watch it. But it is always conquest, conquered and conqueror, for ever. The Kingdom of heaven is the Kingdom of conquerors, who can serve the conquest for ever, after their own conquest is made.

In heaven, in the perfected relation, is peace: in the fourth dimension. But there is getting there. And that, for ever, is the process of conquest.

When the rose blossomed, then the great Conquest was made by the Vegetable Kingdom. But even this conqueror of conquerors, the rose, had to lend himself towards the caterpillar and the butterfly of a later conquest. A conqueror, but tributary to the later conquest.

THE DEATH OF A PORCUPINE

There is no such thing as equality. In the kingdom of heaven, in the fourth dimension, each soul that achieves a perfect relationship with the cosmos, from its own centre, is perfect, and incomparable. It has no superior. It is a conqueror, and incomparable.

But every man, in the struggle of conquest towards his own consummation, must master the inferior cycles of life, and never relinquish his mastery. Also, if there be men beyond him, moving on to a newer consummation than his own, he must yield to their greater demand, and serve their greater mystery, and so be faithful to the kingdom of heaven which is within him, which is gained by conquest and by loyal service.

Any man who achieves his own being will, like the dandelion or the butterfly, pass into that other dimension which we call the fourth, and the old people called heaven. It is the state of perfected relationship. And here a man will have his peace for ever: whether he serve or command, in the process of living.

But even this entails his faithful allegiance to the kingdom of heaven, which must be for ever and for ever extended, as creation conquers chaos. So that my perfection will but serve a perfection which still lies ahead, unrevealed and unconceived, and beyond my own.

We have tried to build walls round the kingdom of heaven: but it's no good. It's only the cabbage rotting inside.

[218]

THE DEATH OF A PORCUPINE

Our last wall is the golden wall of money. This is a fatal wall. It cuts us off from life, from vitality, from the alive sun and the alive earth, as *nothing* can. Nothing, not even the most fanatical dogmas of an iron-bound religion, can insulate us from the inrush of life and inspiration, as money can.

We are losing vitality: losing it rapidly. Unless we seize the torch of inspiration, and drop our money-bags, the moneyless will be kindled by the flame of flames, and they will consume us like old rags.

We are losing vitality, owing to money and money-standards. The torch in the hands of the moneyless will set our house on fire, and burn us to death, like sheep in a flaming corral.

ARISTOCRACY

ARISTOCRACY

EVERYTHING in the world is relative to everything else. And every living thing is related to every other living thing.

But creation moves in cycles, and in degrees. There is higher and lower, in the cycles of creation, and greater and less, in the degree of life.

Each thing that attains to purity in its own cycle of existence, is pure and is itself, and, in its purity, is beyond compare.

But in relation to other things, it is either higher or lower, of greater or less degree.

We have to admit that a daisy is more highly developed than a fern, even if it be a tree-fern. The daisy belongs to a higher order of life. That is, the daisy is more alive. The fern more torpid.

And a bee is more alive than a daisy: of a higher order of life. The daisy, pure as it is in its own being, yet, when compared with the bee, is limited in its being.

And birds are higher than bees: more alive. And

mammals are higher than birds. And man is the highest, most developed, most conscious, most *alive* of the mammals: master of them all.

But even within the species, there is a difference. The nightingale is higher, purer, even more alive, more subtly, delicately alive, than the sparrow. And the parrot is more highly developed, or more alive, than the pigeon.

Among men, the difference in *being* is infinite. And it is a difference in degree as well as in kind. One man *is*, in himself, more, more alive, more of a man, than another. One man has greater being than another, a purer manhood, a more vivid livingness. The difference is infinite.

And, seeing that the inferiors are vastly more numerous than the superiors, when Jesus came, the inferiors, who are no means the meek that they *should* be, set out to inherit the earth.

Jesus, in a world of arrogant Pharisees and egoistic Romans, thought that purity and poverty were one. It was a fatal mistake. Purity is often enough poor. But poverty is only too rarely pure. Poverty too often is only the result of *natural* poorness, poorness in courage, poorness in living vitality, poorness in manhood: poor life, poor character. Now the poor in life are the most impure, the most easily degenerate.

But the few men rich in life and pure in heart read purity into poverty, and Christianity started. "Charity suffereth long, and is kind. Charity envieth not. Charity vaunteth not itself, is not puffed up."

They are the words of a noble manhood.

There happened what was bound to happen: the men with pure hearts left the scramble for money and power to the impure.

Still the great appeal: "The Kingdom of Heaven is within you," acted powerfully on the hearts of the poor, who were still full of life. The rich were more active, but less alive. The poor still wanted, most of all, the Kingdom of Heaven.

Until the pure men began to mistrust the figurative Kingdom of Heaven: "Not much Kingdom of Heaven for a hungry man," they said.

This was a mistake, and a fall into impurity. For even if I die of hunger, the Kingdom of Heaven is within me, and I am within it, if I truly choose.

But once the pure man said this: "*Not much Kingdom of Heaven for a hungry man,*" the Soul began to die out of men.

By the old creed, every soul was equal in the sight of God. By the new creed, every body should be equal in the sight of men. And being equal meant, having equal possessions. And possessions were reckoned in terms of money.

So that money became the one absolute. And man figures as a money-possessor and a money-getter. The absolute, the God, the Kingdom of Heaven itself, became money; hard, hard cash. "The Kingdom of Heaven is within you" now means "The money is in your pocket." "Then shall thy peace be as a river" now means "Then shall thy investments bring thee a safe and ample income."

"*L'homme est né libre*" means "He is born without a sou." "*Et on le trouve partout enchaîné*" means "He wears breeches, and must fill his pockets."

So now there is a new (a new-old) aristocracy, completely unmysterious and scientific: the aristocracy of money. Have you a million *gold*? (for heaven's sake, the gold standard!) Then you are a *king*. Have you five hundred thousand? Then you are a lord.

"In *my* country, we're *all* kings and queens," as the American lady said, being a bit sick of certain British snobbery. She was quite right: they are all potential kings and queens. But until they come into their kingdom—five hundred thousand dollars minimum—they might just as well be commoners.

Yet even still, there is *natural* aristocracy.

Aristocracy of birth is bunk, when a Kaiser Wilhelm and an Emperor Franz-Josef and a Czar Nicolas is all that noble birth will do for you.

Yet the whole of life is established on a natural aristocracy. And aristocracy of birth is a *little* more natural than aristocracy of money. (Oh, for God's sake, the gold standard!)

But a millionaire can do without birth, whereas

birth cannot do without dollars. So, by the all-prevailing law of pragmatism, the dollar has it.

What then does *natural* aristocracy consist in?

It's not just brains! The mind is an instrument, and the *savant*, the professor, the scientist, has been looked upon since the Ptolemies, as a sort of upper servant. And justly. The millionaire has brains too: so does a modern President or Prime Minister. They all belong to the class of upper servants. They serve, forsooth, the public.

"Ca, Ca, Caliban!
Get a new master, be a new man."

What does a natural aristocracy consist in? Count Keyserling says: "Not in what a man can *do*, but what he *is*." Unfortunately what a man *is*, is measured by what he can do, even in nature. A nightingale, being a nightingale, can sing: which a sparrow can't. If you *are* something you'll *do* something, *ipso facto*.

The question is what *kind* of thing can a man do? Can he put more life into us, and release in us the fountains of our vitality? Or can he only help to feed us, and give us money or amusement.

The providing of food, money, and amusement belongs, truly, to the servant class.

The providing of *life* belongs to the aristocrat. If a man, whether by thought or action, makes *life*, he is an aristocrat. So Cæsar and Cicero are both strictly aristocrats. Lacking these two, the first century B.C. would have been far less vital, less vividly alive. And Antony, who seemed so much more vital, robust and robustious, was, when we look at it, comparatively unimportant. Cæsar and Cicero lit the flame.

How? It is easier asked than answered.

But one thing they did, whatever else: they put men into a new relation with the universe. Cæsar opened Gaul, Germany and Britain, and let the gleam of ice and snow, the shagginess of the north, the mystery of the menhir and the mistletoe in upon the rather stuffy soul of Rome, and of the Orient. And Cicero was discovering the moral nature of man, as citizen chiefly, and so putting man in new relation to man.

But Cæsar was greater than Cicero. He put man in new relation to ice and sun.

Only Cæsar was, perhaps, also too much an egoist; he never knew the mysteries he moved amongst. But Cæsar was great *beyond* morality.

Man's life consists in a connection with all things in the universe. Whoever can establish, or initiate a new connection between mankind and the circumambient universe is, in his own degree, a saviour. Because mankind is always exhausting its human possibilities, always degenerating into repetition, torpor, *ennui*, lifelessness. When *ennui* sets in, it is a sign that human vitality is waning, and the human connection with the universe is gone stale.

Then he who comes to make a new revelation, a new connection, whether he be soldier, statesman, poet, philosopher, artist, he is a saviour.

When George Stephenson invented the locomotive engine, he provided a *means of communication*, but he didn't alter in the slightest man's *vital* relation to the universe. But Galileo and Newton, *discoverers*, not inventors, they made a big difference. And the energy released in mankind because of them was enormous. The same is true of Peter the Great, Frederick the Great, and Napoleon. The same is true of Voltaire, Shelley, Wordsworth, Byron, Rousseau. They established a *new* connection between mankind and the universe, and the result was a vast release of energy. The *sun* was reborn to man, so was the moon.

To man, the very sun goes stale, becomes a habit. Comes a saviour, a seer, and the very sun dances new in heaven.

That is because the *sun* is always *sun beyond sun beyond sun*. The sun is every sun that ever has been, Helios or Mithras, the sun of China or of Brahma, or of Peru or of Mexico: great gorgeous suns, besides which our puny "envelope of incandescent gas" is a smoky candle-wick.

It is our fault. When man becomes stale and paltry, his sun is the mere stuff that our sun is. When man is

[229]

great and splendid, the sun of China and Mithras blazes over him and gives him, not radiant energy in the form of heat and light, but life, life, life!

The world is to us what we take from it. The sun is to us what we take from it. And if we are puny, it is because we take punily from the superb sun.

Man is great according as his relation to the living universe is vast and vital.

Men are related to men: including women: and this, of course, is very important. But one would think it were everything. One would think, to read modern books, that the life of any tuppenny bank-clerk was more important than sun, moon, and stars; and to read the pert drivel of the critics, one would be led to imagine that every three-farthing whipper-snapper who lifts up his voice in approval or censure were the thrice-greatest Hermes speaking in judgment out of the mysteries.

This is the democratic age of cheap clap-trap, and it sits in jackdaw judgment on all greatness.

And this is the result of making, in our own conceit, man the measure of the universe. Don't you be taken in. The universe, so vast and profound, measures man up very accurately, for the yelping mongrel with his tail between his legs, that he is. And the great sun, and the moon, with a smile will soon start dropping the mongrel down the vast refuse-pit of oblivion. Oh, the universe has a terrible hole in the middle of it, an oubliette for all of you, whipper-snappering mongrels.

Man, of course, being measure of the universe, is measured only against man. Has, of course, vital relationship only with his own cheap little species. Hence the cheap little twaddler he has become.

In the great ages, man had vital relation with man, with woman: and beyond that, with the cow, the lion, the bull, the cat, the eagle, the beetle, the serpent. And beyond these, with narcissus and anemone, mistletoe and oak-tree, myrtle, olive, and lotus. And beyond these with humus and slanting water, cloud-towers and rainbow and the sweeping sun-limbs. And beyond that, with sun, and moon, the living night and the living day.

Do you imagine the great realities, even the ram of Amon, are only *symbols* of something human? Do you imagine the great symbols, the dragon, the snake, the bull, only refer to bits, qualities or attributes of little man? It is puerile. The puerilty, the puppyish conceit of modern white humanity is almost funny.

Amon, the great ram, do you think he doesn't stand alone in the universe, without your permission, oh cheap little man? Because he's there, do you think *you* bred him, out of your own almightiness, you cheap-jack?

Amon, the great ram! Mithras, the great bull! The mistletoe on the tree. Do you think, you stuffy little human fool sitting in a chair and wearing lambs-wool underwear and eating your mutton and beef under the Christmas decoration, do you think then that Amon, Mithras, Mistletoe, and the whole Tree of Life were just invented to contribute to your complacency?

You fool! You dyspeptic fool, with your indigestion tablets! You can eat your mutton and your beef, and by sixpenn'orth of the golden bough, till your belly turns sour, you fool. Do you think, because you keep a fat castrated cat, the moon is upon your knees? Do you think, in your woolen underwear, you are clothed in the might of Amon?

You idiot! You cheap-jack idiot!

Was not the ram created before you were, you twaddler? Did he not come in night out of chaos? And is he not still clothed in might? To you, he is mutton. Your wonderful perspicacity relates you to him just that far. But any farther, he is—well, wool.

Don't you see, idiot and fool, that you have *lost* the ram out of your life entirely, and it is one great connection gone, one great life-flow broken? Don't you see you are so much the emptier, mutton-stuffed and wool-wadded, but lifeless, lifeless.

And the oak-tree, the slow great oak-tree, isn't he alive? Doesn't he live where you don't live, with a vast silence you shall never, never penetrate, though you chop him into kindling shred from shred? He is

[232]

alive with life such as you have not got and will never have. And in so far as he is a vast, powerful, silent life, you should worship him.

You should seek a living relation with him. Didn't the old Englishman have a living, vital relation to the oak-tree, a *mystic* relation? Yes, mystic! Didn't the red-faced old Admirals who *made* England, have a living relation in *sacredness*, with the oak-tree which was their ship, their ark? The last living vibration and power in pure connection, between man and tree, coming down from the Druids.

And all you can do now is to twiddle-twaddle about golden boughs, because you are empty, empty, empty, hollow, deficient, and cardboardy.

Do you think the tree is not, now and for ever, sacred and fearsome? The trees have turned against you, fools, and you are running in imbecility to your own destruction.

Do you think the bull is at your disposal, you zenith of creation? Why, I tell you, the blood of the bull is indeed your poison. Your veins are bursting, with beef. You may well turn vegetarian. But even milk is bull's blood: or Hathor's.

My cow Susan is at my disposal indeed. But when I see her suddenly emerging, jet-black, sliding through the gate of her little corral into the open sun, does not my heart stand still, and cry out, in some long-forgotten tongue, salutation to the fearsome one? Is not even now my life widened and deepened in connection with her life, throbbing with the other pulse, of the bull's blood?

Is not this my life, this throbbing of the bull's blood in my blood?

And as the white cock calls in the doorway, who calls? Merely a barnyard rooster, worth a dollar-and-a-half. But listen! Under the old dawns of creation the Holy Ghost, the Mediator, shouts aloud in the twilight. And every time I hear him, a fountain of vitality gushes up in my body. It is life.

So it is! Degree after degree after degree widens out the relation between man and his universe, till it reaches the sun, and the night.

The impulse of existence, of course, is to *devour* all the lower orders of life. So man now looks upon the white cock, the cow, the ram, as good to eat.

But *living* and having *being* means the relatedness between me and all things. In so far as I am I, a being who is proud and in place, I have a connection with my circumambient universe, and I know my place. When the white cock crows, I do not hear myself, or some anthropomorphic conceit, crowing. I hear the not-me, the voice of the Holy Ghost. And when I see the hard, solid, longish green cones thrusting up at blue heaven from the high bluish tips of the balsam pine, I say: "Behold! Look at the strong, fertile silence of the thrusting tree! God is in the bush like a clenched dark fist, or a thrust phallus."

So it is with every natural thing. It has a vital relation with all other natural things. Only the machine is absolved from vital relation. It is based on the mystery of neuters. The neutralising of one great natural force against another, makes mechanical power. Makes the engine's wheels go round.

Does the earth go round like a wheel, in the same way? No! In the living, balanced, hovering flight of the earth, there is a strange leaning, an unstatic equilibrium, a balance that is non-balance. This is owing to the relativity of earth, moon, and sun, a vital, even sentient relatedness, never perpendicular: nothing neutral or neuter.

Every natural thing has its own living relation to every other natural thing. So the tiger, striped in gold and black, lies and stretches his limbs in perfection between all that the day is, and all that is night. He has a by-the-way relatedness with trees, soil, water, man, cobras, deer, ants, and of course, the she-tiger. Of all these he is reckless as Cæsar was. When he stretches himself superbly, he stretches himself between the living day and the living night, the vast inexhaustible duality of creation. And he is the fanged and brindled Holy Ghost, with ice-shining whiskers.

The same with man. His life consists in a relation with all things: stone, earth, trees, flowers, water, insects, fishes, birds, creatures, sun, rainbow, children, women, other men. But his greatest and final relation is with the sun, the sun of suns: and with the night, which is moon and dark and stars. In the last great connections, he lifts his body speechless to the sun, and, the same body, but so different, to the moon and the stars, and the spaces between the stars.

Sun! Yes, the actual sun! That which blazes in the day! Which scientists call a sphere of blazing gas—what a lot of human gas there is, which has never been set ablaze!—and which the Greeks call Helios!

The sun, I tell you, is alive, and more alive than I am, or a tree is. It may have blazing gas, as I have hair, and a tree has leaves. But I tell you, it is the Holy Ghost in full raiment, shaking and walking, and alive as a tiger is, only more so, in the sky.

And when I can turn my body to the sun, and say: "Sun! Sun!" and we meet—then I am come finally into my own. For the universe of day, finally, is the sun. And when the day of the sun is my day too, I am a lord of all the world.

And at night, when the silence of the moon, and the stars, and the spaces between the stars, is the silence of me too, then I am come into my own by night. For night is a vast untellable life, and the Holy Ghost starry, beheld as we only behold night on earth.

In his ultimate and surpassing relation, man is given only to that which he can never describe or account for; the sun, as it is alive, and the living night.

A man's supreme moment of active life is when he looks up and is with the sun, and is with the sun as a woman is with child. The actual yellow sun of morning.

This makes man a lord, an aristocrat of life.

And the supreme moment of quiescent life is when a man looks up into the night, and is gone into the night, so the night is like a woman with child, bearing him. And this, a man has to himself.

The true aristocrat is the man who has passed all the relationships and has met the sun, and the sun is with him as a diadem.

Cæsar was like this. He passed through the great relationships, with ruthlessness, and came to the sun. And he became a sun-man. But he was too unconscious. He was not aware that the sun for ever was beyond him, and that only in his *relation* to the sun was he deified. He wanted to be God.

Alexander was wiser. He placed himself a god among men. But when blood flowed from a wound in him, he said, "Look! It is the blood of a man like other men."

The sun makes man a lord: an aristocrat: almost a deity. But in his consummation with night and the moon, man knows for ever his own passing away.

But no man is man in all his splendour till he passes

further than every relationship: further than mankind and womankind, in the last leap to the sun, to the night. The man who can touch both sun and night, as the woman touched the garment of Jesus, becomes a lord and a saviour, in his own kind. With the sun he has his final and ultimate relationship, beyond man or woman, or anything human or created. And in this final relation is he most intensely alive, surpassing.

Every creature at its zenith surpasses creation and is alone in the face of the sun, and the night: the sun that lives, and the night that lives and survives. Then we pass beyond every other relationship, and every other relationship, even the intensest passion of love, sinks into subordination and obscurity. Indeed, every relationship, even that of purest love, is only an approach nearer and nearer, to a man's last consummation with the sun, with the moon or night. And in the consummation with the sun, even love is left behind.

He who has the sun in his face, in his body, he is the pure aristocrat. He who has the sun in his breast, and the moon in his belly, he is the first: the aristocrat of aristocrats, supreme in the aristocracy of life.

Because he is *most alive*.

Being alive constitutes an aristocracy which there is no getting beyond. He who is most alive, intrinsically, is King, whether men admit it or not. In the face of the sun.

ARISTOCRACY

Life rises in circles, in degrees. The most living is the highest. And the lower shall serve the higher, if there is to be any life among men.

More life! More *vivid* life! Not more safe cabbages, or meaningless masses of people.

Perhaps Dostoevsky was more vividly alive than Plato: culminating a more vivid life circle, and giving the clue towards a higher circle still. But the clue *hidden*, as it always is hidden, in every revelation, underneath what is stated.

All creation contributes, and must contribute to this: towards the achieving of a vaster, vivider cycle of life. That is the goal of living. He who gets nearer the sun is leader, the aristocrat of aristocrats. Or he who, like Dostoevsky, gets nearest the moon of our not-being.

There is, of course, the power of mere conservatism and inertia. Deserts made the cactus thorny. But the cactus still is a rose of roses.

Whereas a sort of cowardice made the porcupine spiny. There is a difference between the cowardice of inertia, which now governs the democratic masses, particularly the capitalist masses: and the conservative fighting spirit which saved the cactus in the middle of the desert.

The democratic mass, capitalist and proletariat alike, are a vast, sluggish, ghastlily greedy porcupine, lumbering with inertia. Even Bolshevism is the same porcupine: nothing but greed and inertia.

ARISTOCRACY

The cactus had a rose to fight for But what has democracy to fight for, against the living elements, except money, money, money!

The world is stuck solid inside an achieved form, and bristling with a myriad spines, to protect its hulking body as it feeds: gnawing the bark of the young tree of Life, and killing it from the top downwards. Leaving its spines to fester and fester in the nose of the gay dog.

The actual porcupine, in spite of legend, cannot shoot its quills. But mankind, the porcupine outpigging the porcupine, can stick quills into the face of the sun.

Bah! Enough of the squalor of democratic humanity. It is time to begin to recognize the aristocracy of the sun. The children of the sun shall be lords of the earth.

There will form a new aristocracy, irrespective of nationality, of men who have reached the sun. Men of the sun, whether Chinese or Hottentot, or Nordic, or Hindu, or Esquimo, if they touch the sun in the heavens, are lords of the earth. And together they will form the aristocracy of the world. And in the coming era they will rule the world; a confraternity of the living sun, making the embers of financial internationalism and industrial internationalism pale upon the hearth of the earth.